‘Tom, you’ve been so good to me.’

She leaned forward, gently kissed him. She had intended it just to be a friendly goodnight kiss. But on the lips. And then, somehow, she didn’t move. They remained there, only their lips touching. And after a moment she put her hands on his shoulders and closed her eyes. She felt his arms round her, bringing her towards him. There was such comfort in the touch of his body against hers that she wanted to stay there for ever. She didn’t need to think of anything now. She was safe.

‘You’re not to let me go now. Please, Tom, I need you.’

Dear Reader

Of all the departments in a large modern hospital, perhaps the most exciting, most difficult, most rewarding, must be the maternity section. What responsibility could be greater than knowing that only your skill and training can bring a new life into the world? What thrill could be greater than seeing proud parents carry away the child that you have helped be born?

The three heroines of these books are all dedicated to their work. They are trained in all aspects of maternity care—ante-natal, post-natal, delivery suite, SCBU and clinic. They find their careers deeply satisfying. But they are also young healthy women, who need further fulfilment outside work.

Sometimes it is difficult to separate your private and your work life. A hospital can be like a glasshouse, where emotions and feelings grow faster, grow more intense. My three midwives all think they have found love in the hospital—but there are problems. Work and love become interwined, and it is difficult to sort out priorities, to decide exactly what feelings mean.

Love will always find a way. Our heroines find that that way can be a hard one—but in the end they triumph.

I hope you enjoy reading these stories; I enjoyed writing them.

Best wishes

Gill Sanderson

Look out for the next story
set in **Dell Owen Maternity—**
THE NOBLE DOCTOR—coming next month
from Mills & Boon® Medical Romance™

A CHILD TO CALL HER OWN

BY

GILL SANDERSON

MILLS & BOON®

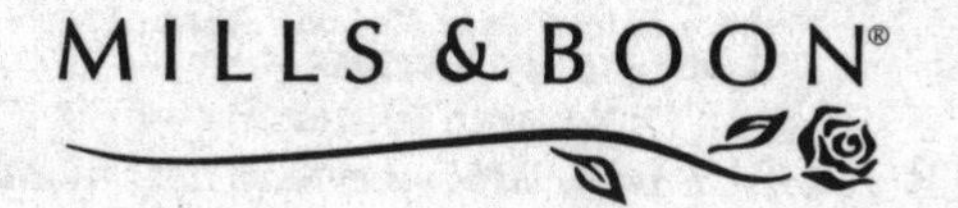

All the characters in this book have no existence outside the imagination of the author, and have no relation whatsoever to anyone bearing the same name or names. They are not even distantly inspired by any individual known or unknown to the author, and all the incidents are pure invention.

First published in Great Britain 2005
Harlequin Mills & Boon Limited,
Eton House, 18-24 Paradise Road, Richmond, Surrey TW9 1SR

ISBN 0 263 84342 4

Set in Times Roman 10½ on 12½ pt.
03-1105-44196

Printed and bound in Spain
by Litografia Rosés, S.A., Barcelona

CHAPTER ONE

MIDWIFE Maria Wyatt was having a nightmare.

It didn't happen so often now, perhaps once a month instead of two or three times a week. More than one doctor had told her that the dreams would pass, that time would heal everything. It hadn't healed her so far. The dreams were more rare, but still as bad.

She woke sobbing, whimpering, her pillow wet with tears and her body damp with sweat. And the images disappeared. A pity really, some of them had brought her so much happiness. A baby in a cot, a child taking his first steps, the same child a year older, smiling at the camera. But then there had been the others.

She looked at the red figures on her bedside clock. It was five in the morning, the room dark. No daylight for three hours yet, it was January. Maria lay there, her breathing slowly getting calmer, her pumping heart slowing.

Today was the beginning of a new era in her career as a midwife. It was a pity to start it with a nightmare.

There was no way she would get back to sleep. She climbed wearily out of bed, pulled on her dressing-gown and walked into the corridor of the nurses' home. Just a chance that there might be somebody to talk to. But there was no one. She'd have to get through this alone. This was usual, she'd done it before.

Since she was in the kitchen, she made herself a mug of tea. Then she went back to her room to sit on the bed and try to think positive thoughts. The good thing was that she knew that in time the horror would pass. But first there was something she had to do.

She slid open the bottom drawer of the built-in unit, felt under the layers of carefully stored summer clothes and took out a thick album. She had to keep it hidden. She didn't want it on view, where people might open it, ask her questions.

For perhaps ten minutes she stared at just one photograph. It was of herself, and she was holding a baby. She looked at the picture of her own, younger face. Then she glanced into her dressing-table mirror. There was a world of difference between her features now and how they had been just six short years ago.

Then, decisively, she snapped the album shut. Life had to go on. She had a new job to think of.

She sat on her bed, opened the heavy midwifery textbook on her bedside table. As she flicked through it she saw pressed flowers. Pressing flowers was something she had done as a child—and had never quite got out of the habit. But these were not wild flowers. They were maroon and lemon roses. Maria had been a bridesmaid to her friend and tutor, Jenny Carson—now Jenny Donovan—and the flowers were from Jenny's bouquet. Maria smiled at the memory. Life wasn't all bad.

She read in bed for an hour and then showered and dressed. She put on her new community midwife uniform, which she rather liked. On the ward in hospital she had worn either scrubs or the usual midwife's blue. This uniform was slightly more formal. More useful for home visits.

Technically, she was still working for the hospital trust but she was on outreach. The hospital had opened a couple of clinics in distant parts of the city, dealing mostly with pregnancy and the welfare of younger children. Maria was to work at the Landmoss clinic.

It had only been four months since Maria had qualified as a midwife so this job should have gone to someone more experienced. But the midwife originally appointed had broken her leg in a fall, she'd be off work for at least six months. So Jenny had suggested Maria. 'Good experience and you're a bit older than the other possibilities,' she had told Maria. 'I know you can do it.'

'I'd like the job,' Maria had said after a minute's thought. 'I fancy working in a clinic for a while. But it's just O and G, isn't it? Just mums and babies. No small kids?'

'No small kids,' Jenny had said, looking levelly at her charge, 'not unless you want to work with them.'

'I don't. Well, not yet anyway. Perhaps in a year or two I'll change my mind…but for now I'm happy as a midwife.'

'A year or two?' Jenny had said quietly. 'Don't leave it too late, will you?'

Maria had shrugged. 'I'm improving,' she said. 'It doesn't hurt as much. Not quite as much.'

'Good. There is another thing, though. The doctor in charge will want to see your CV. He'll learn about your son.'

There had been silence between them. Then Maria had muttered, 'You'd better tell him, then. And about how I feel.'

Jenny had reached over, clasped her friend's hand. Then her voice had altered, become efficient again. 'There's another thing I should warn you of. A lot of the time you'll be out on your own. Here in the hospital there's always help at hand. But out on the streets things can get unpleasant—violent even. Can you cope with that?'

'I can cope. You know I'm tough.'

Jenny had looked at her speculatively. 'You are in some ways. But anyway...you'll be working with one of our O and G specialist registrars—a Dr Tom Ramsey. He's a good man. Just don't call him Blondie.'

'What?' Maria hadn't quite been able to read Jenny's half-amused expression.

'It's just that he's got blond hair,' Jenny had said. 'It's quite something. I think the two of you will get on together.' So it had been settled.

Maria had one last glance in the mirror, smoothed down her super-short dark hair. Her midwife's bag was ready packed at the foot of the bed. From now on she'd never move without it.

First day at a new job. It wouldn't hurt to arrive early.

It was cold out, just getting light. Christmas was now over, she could look forward to the depths of winter. There was a little notebook on the dashboard of her car, from now on she could claim a mileage allowance. That was something new.

Memories of the nightmare were now fading. She was setting off to start a new life.

The Landmoss Clinic was a new building about six miles from the hospital. It was set in a vast estate of new houses, many of them occupied by first-time buyers—people proud of their new homes and tending to be starting families. But there were also three large tower blocks, many of the flats there occupied by what were tactfully called 'problem' families.

'There'll be a lot of teenage pregnancies,' Jenny had told her. 'It'll be your job to make sure they get the care they'll need. You'll meet a lot of interesting people.'

'All babies are interesting to me. And I love them.'

It was an easy ride to the clinic as most of the traffic was heading into the city. She turned into the leafy avenue that led to the clinic, glancing sideways at a small shopping centre. And frowned.

A crowd of people was gathered on the pavement, apparently looking down at something—or someone. There was something about their attitude that suggested there had been an accident. Someone was lying on the pavement. Maria was not a registered nurse, but she had some medical training and she might be able to help. And it wasn't in her character just to move on by.

She stopped the car, took her midwife's bag. It held a few medical supplies that might be useful. She approached the group, saw that there was indeed someone lying on the ground. Firmly she said, 'Could you let me through, please? I might be able to help.' The people parted.

A panicking voice said, 'He just walked in front of my car. There was nothing I could do. I knocked him into that lamppost.'

Maria looked up, saw a young man and noticed that he had a mobile phone in a holder on his belt. 'Phone 999,' she said. 'Do it now. Ask for an ambulance.' Then she looked at the victim.

He was an old man, apparently unconscious, lying on his back on the pavement, blood in his hair. Someone had thrown a coat over him, another man was kneeling and was about to lift up the old man's head. Sharply, Maria said, 'Don't lift his head! Let it down where it was, very carefully. We need to check for a broken neck.'

Gently, the man lowered the head, and then stood back. He was obviously glad to hand over responsibility.

Maria knelt by the old man, tried to remember her first aid. ABC. Check airways, breathing, circulation. Quickly done. The man might be unconscious but he was still alive. She lifted the coat but could see no signs of excessive bleeding—the head injury was the worst. She opened her bag, almost automatically pulled on a pair of latex gloves. Then she took out a sterile pad. Technically it was used to stop vaginal bleeding—but it would do.

She didn't like the angle of the man's neck. But there was no hard collar in her midwife's bag.

Behind her a voice asked, 'Are you a doctor?' It wasn't an anxious voice but firm and assured, a voice that gave confidence.

Without looking round, she answered, 'No, I'm a midwife. Just doing what I can.'

'Well, I'm a doctor. Would you like me to take over?'

Taking her agreement as read, a man knelt by her side. Jenny glanced at him—and gasped.

She remembered that Jenny had told her that the O and G doctor at the clinic would be a Dr Tom Ramsey—and that she was not to call him Blondie. Well, this had to be the man. But his hair wasn't blond, it was spun gold. He wore it fairly long and it was wavy. Even at that cold hour of the morning, even as they looked at an emergency together, she wanted to run her hands through it to feel if it was as soft as it looked.

Then he turned to look at her and she gasped again. If anything, his face was more striking than his... Then she collected herself. He wasn't smiling. This wasn't a social meeting, he had a job to do—as did she.

'I've sent for an ambulance, I've checked ABC,' she said. 'Now may I help you in any way?'

He was feeling the back of the unconscious man's neck, his fingers delicate as they traced down the line of vertebrae. 'Look in my bag,' he said. 'There's a hard collar there. We'll get that on him and then just wait for the ambulance.'

He had placed his bag by his side and it took her only a minute to find the collar. Then she slid it round the old man's neck as the doctor carefully raised his head.

'At a guess, you'll be Midwife Maria Wyatt,' he said when they had finished. 'I'm Tom Ramsey and I've been looking forward to meeting you.'

'Yes, I'm Maria Wyatt.'

'Well, there's nothing much more we can do here until the ambulance arrives. But just to be certain, I'm going to stay with the man. You can do me a favour, though.'

'Anything I can.'

He nodded in the direction of a parked blue car. 'My four-year-old son James is in that car. He's upset, he's just seen a bit too much. Could you take him to the clinic for me? I'll come and pick him up later, he's in the crèche there.'

Maria flinched. 'I'm a midwife, not an expert on small boys,' she said. 'Can't I help here? I'd rather do that.'

He looked at her in surprise. 'There's nothing you can do here now,' he said. 'There is something you can do to help a small distressed boy, and that is take him to the clinic.' Then he seemed to think. 'Of course, I'm being silly. He'll be fine in the car. You stay here with me.'

Maria stood and dusted the dirt off her skirt. 'You're right. It'd be better if I took him,' she said. 'We'll see you later. I'll take him in my car.'

She told herself there was nothing to it, just babysit a small child for a few minutes. Anyone could do it easily. Anyone but her. She gritted her teeth, she would much rather have helped the doctor. But the job was hers now.

She opened the back door of the doctor's car, looked at the boy who was securely strapped into his seat by his safety belt. It took an effort but she managed a smile. 'Hi, I'm Maria. What's your name? Your dad's a bit busy right now, he wants me to take you to the clinic in my car.'

The boy was doubtful. 'I'm James,' he said. 'And I'm not supposed to go away with strangers.'

'Of course not. Which is why we're going to walk over together to see him and he can say it's OK.'

She took James's hand, hoping he couldn't tell that hers was trembling. The doctor looked up as they approached and nodded to Maria. 'You go with the lady, James. I'll be with you in a few minutes.'

Now he had permission, James was happier. He grinned up at Maria, squeezed her hand. 'Right, Dad. Is that man going to be all right?'

'He'll be fine if he isn't bothered. Now, off you go.'

Maria managed to unbuckle the child seat from the doctor's car, strapped it in her own car and then secured James in it. Most road accidents happened within five minutes of home.

Then she set off. This was not the way she had anticipated starting her first day at the clinic and she felt anxious. She had specified that she was a midwife, would do ante-natal and post-natal work. As far as was possible, she would deal with the local home births. But she would not be asked to deal with the young children who came into the clinic. Twenty-eight days after babies had been discharged from hospital, they passed out of her care.

All right, this was an emergency. But she'd had nothing to do with young children for over four years now. And that's the way it had to be.

She parked in her slot in the clinic car park, looked around and smiled. It was a new, attractive, red-brick single-storey building. But then she sighed when she saw the ornamental but sturdy bars over the windows. There were drug addicts everywhere, who would thieve anything.

Maria had set off early, hoping to look around her little empire and check on her stocks, work out some kind of programme for the day. But things had changed. She explained about Tom Ramsey to Molly Jowett, the receptionist. Molly, a calm and efficient, middle-aged woman nodded. She noted the troubled look on James's face.

'There's no one in the crèche yet, but why don't

you go down there and let James show you around? Here's the keys. I'll fetch you a coffee and some juice for James.'

'Seems a good idea.' Maria had hoped to hand over James at once but... This time he took her hand and pulled her along the corridor.

'You've been to the crèche before, James?'

'For a few days now. Daddy's brought me.'

'Doesn't your mummy ever bring you?'

'I haven't got a mummy. She died.'

Maria cringed. There had been a time when she wouldn't have made that mistake. She could like James, he had that reserve and dignity possessed by some young children. Now she had to be professional. And if this was not a bit of the profession that she wanted... Well, too bad. It would only be for a while.

'I think you've been a little boy long enough,' she told James. 'How would you like to be a frog?'

A green-faced James crouched in the corner of the room. 'I'm a hungry frog,' he shouted to Maria. 'I can see a fly. I'm going to do a frog jump and catch him with my tongue!'

With a very able representation of a frog jump, he leapt into the centre of the room and stuck out his tongue. Then he shouted again. 'Daddy!'

Maria put down the pot of green face paint and turned. There in the doorway was the tall figure she now knew to be Dr Tom Ramsey.

He had taken off his coat and jacket and her first

impression was of his white shirt contrasting with the gold of his hair. Now there was no emergency, now they weren't kneeling together on a cold road, she could look at him more carefully. Quite simply, her new boss was the most attractive man she had met in years. To her surprise she realised that her heart was beating a little faster. She didn't usually react this way.

He was smiling, not at her but at his son. For a moment she wished that she had someone who would smile at her like that. But the moment passed. She was all right.

'A frog?' he said to James. 'Well, then, I'm a bigger, better frog.'

To Maria's surprise—and delight—he crouched down himself and in three giant bounds leapt towards his son. 'Not many flies around today, are there?' he asked. James collapsed in giggles.

Tom walked back to speak to Maria. 'I think his face is wonderful,' he said, 'and so does he. You must be used to doing this.'

Maria shook her head. 'I just followed a pattern,' she said. 'Anyone could do it.'

'I doubt I could. But I'm sure I'll be asked to try. Has he been all right with you?'

'I think so. We've enjoyed ourselves together.'

Tom nodded. 'He's been a bit doubtful about coming to the crèche—I was a bit doubtful, too, about bringing him. But now I know you're here and he can have a good time with you, I'm sure he'll be happier.'

Maria shook her head—this had to be discouraged.

'I'll see him around, I suppose,' she said, 'but I'm primarily here as a midwife. I expect I'll have a lot to do.' She thought it a good idea to move on to some other topic. 'How was the man who was knocked down?'

'I handed him over to the paramedics. I think you were right, by the way. I suspect there was damage to the spine. It was a good thing you stopped him being moved.'

'I'm glad to have been of help. Now you're here, so if I can hand James over to you I'd like to look around my room, check the stocks and records and so on.'

She looked around the crèche, saw the toys, the children's paintings on the wall. Too many memories. She needed to get out of the crèche.

He looked at her searchingly then glanced at the pictures himself. There was silence for a moment and then he said, 'Of course. Mrs Roberts, who runs the crèche, will be here in a few minutes. I'll have James in my room till then. If you'd like to come to my office in, say, an hour, we could run over what you'll be doing here.'

'Of course, Doctor,' she said. Now was the time for formality.

Perhaps Maria had been lucky, but all the doctors she had worked with at the Dell Owen Hospital had been both competent and helpful. She had got on well with them all—even been out with a couple of the younger ones. Not that anything had come of it. She just didn't need any kind of intense relationship.

Now she was working with another doctor. It so happened that she'd never met him before. She was sure he'd be a good doctor. But for reasons she couldn't quite force herself to admit, she found him disturbing.

This was silly! She couldn't fall for a doctor on her first day working with him. And normally she was happy and busy with her work, she didn't seem to have much time for men. But he was so attractive—that blond hair, the rugged, thoughtful face... She shrugged, unlocked the first filing cabinet in her office and started to check through the latest case notes. She was here to work.

In exactly an hour she knocked on his door. She knew that this was a relationship she had to get right. In the hospital there had been a variety of doctors and if she didn't get on with one then it hadn't mattered too much. But she'd have to work closely with this man. It was important that they got things right from the start. That he knew what she could and what she could not do.

She thought she had got into the right frame of mind when she heard his invitation to come in. She would be composed, professional, attentive. But when she opened the door, saw his face light up and that wonderful, wonderful gold hair—well, things seemed a bit different.

He stood, offered her his hand and smiled. 'It seems

that we've been working together already,' he said, 'and working very well, too. But now may I formally welcome you to the clinic. I'm Dr Tom Ramsey. Sometimes we'll have to be formal—I suggest "Midwife" and "Doctor". But I hope you'll call me Tom and you're...Maria, is it?'

'Yes, Maria.' She nodded. 'It's good to meet you...Tom.'

Tom waved her to a seat, sat down himself. 'I hope you'll be happy here,' he said. 'Personally, I'm very glad to see you, we need a midwife desperately. And James is happy you're here, too. I worried about him settling in here, but you've made it easier for him.'

'He seems a nice little boy,' Maria said. She knew she had to be cautious here, be tactful. 'But I don't think I'll see too much of him. I've just qualified, I'm still learning. I want to concentrate on midwifery, not...not paediatrics.'

She knew what she had said had been clumsy and hoped desperately that this man wouldn't mind too much. She wanted to work with him. But she had to indicate to him that in no way could she become a particular friend to James.

'That's very understandable,' he said after a moment. 'And I like people who know what they have to do. Now, three times a week we'll work together when I run a clinic. I'll be here most of the rest of the time, but you'll be on your own, running the ante-natal and the post-natal classes, making home visits and all the usual checks. But, remember, we are a team. You can interrupt me at any time if you have a query. And I'll do the same with you. Happy with that?'

'Very happy,' she said.

'There'll be things you need to know in the next few days, the way we work and so on. I'm afraid that as yet I haven't written any kind of formal induction programme. I'd like to write one. Perhaps, when we get this clinic fully organised, we could work on it together?'

'I'd like that,' she said.

'But until one is written—as I said—drop in any time.'

The interview seemed to be at an end. At this stage there was nothing more they had to say to each other, but she didn't want to go. And for some reason she felt that he didn't want her to go either. It was something unspoken, but they seemed to feel happy just to be with each other

She sat there a while longer. Then, perhaps a little sadly, she said, 'I suppose I'd better go. I've got my first set of new mums coming in half an hour.'

'Fine. But, remember, I'm always here.'

Maria hurried to her room, checked over the notes for her first visitor and set out the trolley with everything she would need. Ten minutes to wait. She thought about her new boss.

It wasn't right that a man should have hair like that! And it was even longer than hers—though she had had hers cut brutally short. And inevitably he had the blue eyes to go with the golden hair. Large, dark blue eyes. He didn't have a pretty or feminine face. He had a tough face. For quite a young man there were more lines than she would have expected. It was the face of a man who could take decisions, no matter what the consequences.

She had noticed that after the first welcoming smile he hadn't smiled too much. He was pleasant but there was a reserve there. Well, reserve was good. James had said that his mother had died. Maria wondered how and when that had happened. Not that she could ask, of course.

Tom was a fit man, too. Maria could tell by the way he walked, by the trimness of his waist. Altogether, a very attractive man. The kind of man she would like to see more of. But she could not. For the moment, Maria felt she just couldn't cope with a four-year-old boy, especially one as sweet as James. Somehow she had managed this morning. But it was a situation to be avoided.

Maria forced herself to stop thinking about Tom and concentrated on the notes for her first patient.

It might have surprised her to know that Tom was thinking just as hard about her.

Maria had come very well recommended. Tom had asked for someone mature, who had several years in the profession, who was experienced. Ideally, someone who had children of her own. Jenny had told him that Maria was as good as anyone who had been working as a midwife for years. And she had told him things about Maria's past that had made him instantly sympathetic.

Unconsciously, he realised, he had still been half expecting a motherly, middle-aged woman. Instead he had got a tall, willowy beauty with penetrating grey eyes and a mouth that gave him feelings that he hadn't known in years. A pity her dark hair was cut so severely. But she was a beauty. He shook his head. His life was complicated enough already.

Maria had a good morning. At first it was a little difficult, she wasn't quite sure where everything was, and of course all the people she saw were new to her. But it was work she had done before, work she enjoyed, and there seemed to be more time to talk individually to her patients. There was no sense of being in some kind of people machine, as there occasionally was in hospital. This work was more intimate. And she liked it.

She had finished by twelve and already had a list of questions she wanted to put to Tom. Nothing too troublesome, just little matters of procedure she wanted to sort out. So she went to his office again.

'Maria! How has the first morning gone?' He seemed very pleased to see her. He pushed aside the pile of papers he was working on, stood and waved her to a chair.

'It's gone well. Just a few little details I want to sort out with you. For a start, there's a couple of patients I'd like you to look at some time. Nothing serious but…'

It took them perhaps ten minutes to sort out her queries. There were no major problems. She enjoyed talking to him, working towards solutions with him. And when everything was finished she felt again that she didn't really want to leave. But… 'Well, that all seems fine,' she said, rather reluctantly. 'I'd better leave you to get on with things.'

'No need to rush off—unless you have to. I thought we might chat a while.'

'I'm always ready to chat,' she said lightly. 'What do you want to talk about?'

He looked apprehensive. 'I want to be straightforward with you,' he said. 'Jenny told me that you had a little boy, and that he died. I wanted you to know that I know. And I sympathise more than you can imagine.'

Maria sat silent. She liked him for his honesty, that he could bring things out into the open. 'There's not much to say,' she said. 'Just so you understand that little boys make me remember. And it hurts.'

'I can see that.' He didn't say anything for a moment, and she found herself searching those dark blue eyes. There was sympathy there, and she thought that she could see a sadness, an acknowledgement that he had suffered, too.

He gave her a wry look. 'You think it'll get easier,' he said, 'you think the pain will go in time. Well, perhaps it does. In time.'

Then he smiled at her, and the effect was astounding. The sadness they had just shared was banished. There were other, better things in life.

'Now, let's start on something different,' he said. 'Why did you want to be a midwife?'

'Easy answer. My son was ill in a Spanish hospital and I got to know a lot of the nurses there. They seemed devoted to the job and they seemed to get a kick out of it. So when…when my son died, I wanted to do something similar myself. Not to repay anything, you understand, but to get a similar joy myself.'

'But why midwifery?'

'Well, I wondered what kind of medicine I'd like best. And I thought of the one branch of medicine where most of the time there was a happy ending. I love seeing the joy on a woman's face when she sees her child for the first time. Having my son was the best thing that ever happened to me.'

'I know the feeling,' he said.

There was silence for a moment, but both were happy with it.

'I don't talk to many people,' she said.

'Sometimes it helps.'

She tried to get her thoughts in order, to work out what to tell him, what was not really relevant. 'I had a baby just before my nineteenth birthday,' she said. 'A baby boy.'

He nodded.

'I was young and stupid, the father disappeared and now I can barely remember his face. I had my baby, and I was determined to keep him. It was hard, but somehow I managed. And after a while things improved for me. I got a job in Majorca as a kiddie rep for a holiday firm, I could do that and look after my baby. I had a tiny apartment in a hotel. The Hotel

Helena. I had friends to help me and I loved the work and I got promoted. For three years I was happy.'

She drank water from the glass he had poured her, the words were sticking in her throat. 'These are the bare facts,' she said, 'I don't need sympathy and I don't need help.'

'I'll remember that.'

'My son developed a neuroblastoma. It was a rare case, in the brain. By the time the doctors realised that there was something seriously wrong it had spread to the spinal column and the bone marrow. There was no hope of surgery so the hospital tried the usual drugs, vincristine and so on. But we all knew that only a miracle could save him. And we didn't get one. He took six months to die.'

'He was just James's age,' Tom whispered. 'I can imagine what you felt.'

Looking at his sorrowful face, she suspected that perhaps he could imagine her pain.

'And so now you find it hard to deal with young children?' he asked.

'I find it difficult. I'm fine with babies, I love them. But when they're three, four years old…I look at them and I think of my son. And that hurts more than I can tell you.' She smiled bitterly. 'One last thing. My son was called James, too.'

For a moment they stared at each other in silence. Then, to Tom's obvious irritation, his phone rang. And to Maria's relief, it was obviously an important call. 'I'll leave you,' she whispered, and made her escape.

* * *

Back in her own little office she wondered just what she had done. So few people knew about her dead son—she had rarely talked about it. Why had she suddenly decided to confide in Tom—a man she had only just met?

She had to admit it—she was attracted to him. That was as much as she would admit to herself. Just attracted to him. Not merely because he was the best-looking man she'd met in years. There was some feeling between them that she couldn't define. Some mysterious force pulling them together. It was as if they were soul mates. And soul mates shared things.

Then she told herself she was just being fanciful.

That afternoon Maria went to visit one of her new patients who had decided to have her baby at home. Having your baby at home was fairly common—Maria wasn't sure whether she approved or not. Certainly it was often a comfort to the mother—hospitals could be impersonal places. But for a midwife it was good to know that, if something should go wrong, there was expert help available within a couple of minutes.

She pulled up outside number 43 Lashmere Close. It was a new little house down a cul-de-sac in the middle of the housing estate.

As it was winter, the garden was bare, but Maria saw that the fallen leaves had been brushed up, the shrubs and lawn kept very tidy.

As she walked up the path she noted the pristine new net curtains, the highly polished brass doorknob and letterbox. This was a very well-kept house.

Inside all the furniture was new, neat and also polished. And the thirty-eight weeks pregnant Sally Chester was as neat and as organised as her new house. She insisted before they start that she fetch Maria a cup of tea. Tea came on a tray spread with a white embroidered cloth. There were biscuits on a plate, and smaller plates to put them on. And there were napkins.

Maria couldn't help wondering what Sally would do when she had to cope with the inevitably messy business of having a baby.

'This is the first real home of my own,' Sally said, a glint of determination in her eyes. 'I've always wanted a home and a family together, so I decided to begin by having my baby at home, and Brian, my husband, agrees. Other people have tried to put me off the idea. You're not going to do that, are you?'

'Just so long as you understand the risks and the difficulties,' Maria said. 'But I've looked through your notes and everything seems to be going well.'

'We can have a look at the nursery in a minute. I've had it painted in pink and light blue stripes, 'cos we don't care if it's a boy or a girl.'

'Very nice,' said Maria. 'But I'm more interested in the bedroom where you intend to give birth.'

'Well, we have an *en suite* bathroom. Brian has moved all the extra furniture into the spare room so there'll be plenty of room for you to work. And Brian will make us tea and coffee as we want it.'

'You seem to have thought of everything,' Maria

said faintly. 'Now, can we go up to this bedroom? I'd like to examine you.'

'Of course. But would you like another digestive biscuit first?'

There was the usual examination. Perhaps the most important part was the general chatting, so that Maria could assess just how confident and ready Sally was. Then she checked BP, pulse and temperature, felt the lie of the baby, the size and whether the head was engaging. All the signs seemed to suggest that everything was fine.

With a hidden smile, Maria doubted that any new arrival would be allowed to upset Sally's carefully laid plans.

So far Sally had been the perfect mother-to-be. Perhaps the birth would be absolutely straightforward. But Maria wondered if underneath all the careful organisation, the calmness, the perfect control, there might be a problem. Sally was just too good to be true.

She didn't go back to the clinic after her visit, instead went straight back to the nurses' home. As she thought back over her day she decided that she was going to love this kind of work. By their nature, hospitals tended to be enclosed institutions. Being a community midwife meant she was out more in the real world. And she liked that.

She also thought about Dr Tom Ramsey. She thought she was going to enjoy working with him. She wondered again why she had chosen to confide in him—but it was not something she now regretted. She trusted him. And that was as far as she would allow herself to think.

CHAPTER TWO

AFTER four days working at the clinic Maria was even more certain that she enjoyed the work. She wasn't part of a team of midwives any more, she was the only one. Tom had evidently decided to leave her to it, apparently content that she would ask him if she needed help. So she made most of her own decisions and that made her feel wanted and trusted. The second thing that made her content was that the work was so varied. Every day seemed to bring something new.

And there was a good staff. Molly Jowett, the receptionist, knew everybody and almost everything. She had been receptionist at the old clinic before this new one had been built. The lady who ran the crèche, June Roberts, was also friendly. She dropped in to see Maria and asked for a lesson in face-painting. Maria pleaded pressure of work, said she would do it later. On her own she had somehow managed with James, although it had been a strain. But she couldn't face the idea of working with a class full of young children.

Tom was pleasant, too. He always put his head round her door to say good morning. He dropped in from time to time during the day. He never referred to what she had told him, and she was glad. She had confided in him, told him things about herself that few people knew. She didn't mind him knowing, but felt that perhaps they ought to get to know each other better. She had always been cautious with people.

On her second day there he brought in a painting that James had done especially for her. It showed the two of them holding hands, walking from the car to the clinic front door. Maria quickly taped it to one of her cupboards.

'You've made a hit there,' Tom said. 'He's hoping to see more of you. But if it's hard for you…?'

'Give me time,' Maria said. 'I'm settling in here but it's still all a bit hectic. I'd like to be friends with him. If I can cope.'

'There's no hurry,' Tom said.

On Friday morning she was bleeped by Sally Chester. All of the patients who were going to give birth at home were supplied with bleepers and told to use them at any time. Maria rang her straight back. Sally was as confident, as in control as ever. She was in labour. Contractions were now ten minutes apart. She had phoned her husband who had previously told his work that he'd be called away, he was coming home now. Perhaps soon would be a good time for Maria to come. 'I'm on my way,' said Maria. If all new mothers could be as efficient as Sally!

Fortunately she had a more or less free afternoon, otherwise she would have had to draft in another midwife from the hospital to take over her work. She collected her bag, put her head round Tom's door and told him where she was going. 'I'll phone for another midwife from hospital to come and help with the delivery,' she said.

There always had to be two midwifes at a home birth.

'From what you've told me, it should all be straightforward,' Tom said. 'I've got every confidence in you.' Then he looked rather troubled. 'Just one thing. Instead of sending for another midwife, would you mind if I came to assist you? Just to assist. I know you're in charge and I have no intention of taking over.'

Maria was surprised. 'Of course you can come if you want. But you don't know something that I ought to know, do you? Is Sally in any kind of danger?'

He shook his head vigorously. 'No, nothing like that, nothing at all. Every now and again I just like to observe a perfectly normal birth. Will you phone me when you think there's about half an hour to go?'

'Whatever you want,' said Maria.

In fact, she was rather annoyed at Tom's request. This was her birth—he wasn't needed. Was he checking up on her? He certainly hadn't done so yet. Still, if he wanted to assist, he could. If Sally agreed.

She arrived at the neat house and was let in by Brian. This was the first time Maria had met him. He was wearing the apron that midwives suggested that husbands should wear—and underneath it Maria could see a perfectly white shirt and some kind of college tie.

'I have been helping my wife relax by holding her hand and comforting her,' he told Maria. 'The contractions are now three minutes apart and the waters have broken. I understand that I have to be in the room to reassure Sally with my presence.'

Maria smiled to herself. Word for word, Brian was quoting from the sheet of suggestions and instructions that the hospital issued to all fathers-to-be.

'Are you looking forward to being a father?' Maria asked.

Brian's mask slipped, just for a moment. 'I'm terrified,' he said.

Maria smiled reassuringly. 'Everything will be fine,' she said, 'and I'll appreciate your help later on.'

She went upstairs and checked Sally. Everything was proceeding well. 'I am managing the pain,' Sally said firmly. 'The relaxation classes were very good and now I am benefiting.'

Another quotation, this time from the little booklet issued to mums-to-be.

If all births were like this, Maria thought once again, her job would be much simpler. But she was still cautious. Sally was too good to be true.

It happened half an hour later. Sally sent Brian downstairs, apparently to ensure that everything was clean and tidy. He did not want to go, protesting that everything was fine and that he wanted to stay. And the book said that he should stay. But Sally was determined. 'We'll call you when we want you,' she said.

Maria felt the first touch of apprehension. There was a quaver in Sally's voice, she wasn't in control any more. And although her contractions were getting more frequent, and more painful, they were still apparently bearable.

She stroked her patient's face. 'Everything's going well,' she soothed. 'It won't be long now and you'll have a beautiful baby.'

'I'm frightened! I've done everything I can and I'm frightened! It'll be like my mother all over again!'

As a matter of course Maria had checked, and had been told that both Sally's parents were dead. Sally had obviously not wanted to talk about them, they had been dismissed at once. But now this. 'What will be like your mother?' Maria asked cautiously.

'My mother wasn't like me. She was a hippie—she carried on smoking and drinking throughout her pregnancy. And then my little brother. He just died, and I know it was her fault and I hated her for it. And now it's going to happen to me. Maria, will I be all right? Will my baby be all right? I've done everything that I should do.'

Maria had wondered at Sally's iron self-control. Now she understood it. It was a reaction against her fear. Whilst offering the world a calm, composed, super-efficient face, underneath she had been terrified. It made her much more human.

'No one could have done more than you,' she reassured, 'and everything is going well. Now, forget about your mother, concentrate on yourself and your husband and your baby. Everything will be fine.'

It took time. But slowly Sally calmed down. Brian came upstairs and, as his instructions said, held her hand and comforted her. Maria sighed with relief.

Labour progressed. In spite of Sally's fears, it was simple and straightforward but still emotionally demanding. A new life coming into the world! Maria felt proud and pleased to be helping.

She had asked Sally's permission, and when she thought the birth was about half an hour away she phoned Tom.

'Get another cup out for the doctor,' Sally gasped.

Tom arrived, was given the almost compulsory cup of tea—and biscuits—served this time by Brian, Maria noticed wryly.

There needed to be two midwives assisting at the moment of birth. Although Tom was an O and G registrar, Maria was in charge. Unless there were problems, the midwife was always in charge.

Tom worked silently with her. Maria had wondered about this, the midwife and her assistant had to work together. They had to guess what was necessary, read each other's thoughts. And she and Tom made an instant, perfect team. That was unusual.

And Maria could sense his pleasure at the work. There was a reverence in his attitude, a gentleness in his hands.

Straightforward but always magical. Maria delivered Sally and Brian's baby. And for the second time Sally lost her iron self-control, 'My baby's been born, my baby's been born!' she screamed. 'Show me my baby!'

'It's a little girl!' Brian gasped, a sob in his voice. 'We've got a daughter.'

It was Tom's job to wrap the baby and then hand

her to Brian, who, as instructed, took the baby and laid it on his wife's breast. A small, perfect little girl.

Maria managed to glance at Tom's face and was struck by what she saw there. She couldn't quite make out his expression—there was half delight, half sadness—but he said nothing, and this was not a time to talk anyway.

The placenta was delivered. After the birth there was a time for, if not relaxation, then calm. Tom quietly left, Brian was sent to make more tea and then bury the placenta where the roses were to be planted. And Sally lay there looking at her child with that expression that Maria had seen so often and loved so much. A kind of contentment, a pride that she had done so well. And an overwhelming feeling of love.

Maria cleared up then she prepared to leave, saying she would return next morning. Brian had the telephone number, to be used for any emergencies. 'I have been told what to expect as normal, and what might be cause for alarm,' Brian said. 'I feel quite confident.' Then his composure broke again. 'Isn't she a gorgeous little girl?'

'She's lovely,' Maria agreed.

As she drove away she wondered with a smile if 43 Lashmere Close would ever be so tidy again.

It wasn't too late so she decided to call at the clinic to write up her report. To her surprise there was a dim light on in Tom's room. She knocked and looked in.

He was working at his desk, sitting in his shirt-sleeves. The screen of his computer shone, there was a small lamp illuminating papers on his desk. His hair glowed golden in the dim light.

He smiled when he saw her. 'Maria, come in and sit down! You must be exhausted.'

'Just a bit now,' she agreed, taking a seat. 'I always get the adrenaline rush when there's a birth—but it's passing now. What are you doing here so late?'

He shrugged. 'Paperwork to catch up on. My mother's come over to look after James for a while. It was a good birth, wasn't it?'

'Perfect,' she agreed. 'I still don't know why you wanted to be there.'

He didn't answer at once. Then he said, 'Being a doctor, you often get called in at awkward times, when there are problems. It's good to remind yourself that the great majority of births are happy, successful events.'

'You seemed quite involved with it,' Maria said.

She sensed some kind of reserve in him and she wasn't entirely convinced by his answer. 'I'm an O and G doctor, Maria. I have to get involved.'

What he said made sense. But once again she couldn't make out his expression. He was looking at her—almost longingly? She didn't know. But although tired she was feeling happy, relaxed. A job had been well done.

She had known him for less than a week, but she felt the afternoon's events had bonded them in some way. And she felt she wanted to see more of him. To see him outside work. She said, 'There's a fundraising event at the hospital social club tomorrow night. Are you going?'

The question hung between them. He looked at her thoughtfully. 'I hadn't intended to,' he said. 'I don't usually go to that kind of function. Will you be going? Are you a party girl?'

'Like you, I don't usually go. But a lot of the department will be there, it'll be a gathering of old friends. We're celebrating Jenny being able to walk again. I want to see that. You know about her accident?'

'I do. And I can envy Mike his good fortune in finding someone like Jenny. They're a couple who deserve happiness.'

'Well,' she went on, 'I'm going to the party. Why don't you drop in, too? If only for a while.'

The desk light illuminated his papers, but left much of his face in shadow. She couldn't see his expression when he said, 'Do you want me to go, Maria? Would it please you to see me there?'

She recognised that this was more than just a casual question. There was a slight tremor in her voice when she said, 'Yes. It would please me to see you there.'

'OK, I'll come. Just for a while. I try to keep as much of my weekends for James, but I'll come to the party after he's gone to sleep.'

'You'll enjoy it,' she promised.

'Look who's just come in!' Jenny Donovan said, 'I never imagined I'd see him at a party.'

Maria was one of a small group of midwifes and

partners happily chatting at the social club. They all turned to see Tom enter.

Seeing him gave Maria a thrill. He looked well—wearing a dark suit with a honey-coloured open-necked shirt—and then that burnished blond hair. Theirs was not the only group to notice him. More than a few heads turned for an apparently casual glance. He was a good-looking man.

'Maria, you're working with him. Did you have anything to do with him coming?' Jenny asked.

'I did tell him there was a party,' Maria admitted. She didn't want to tell anyone that she had persuaded Tom to come. 'Doesn't he go out much?'

'Rarely,' said Jenny. 'He spends most of his time with his son.'

'I'm going to ask him if he wants to join us,' Maria said. 'He doesn't seem to want to join any particular group. We wouldn't want him to feel lonely.'

Her cheeks warmed as she felt Jenny's appraising glance. 'He doesn't look lonely,' Jenny said. 'But do go and ask him.'

Jenny was right, Maria thought as she looked at Tom. He seemed quite cool and collected as he made his way towards the bar.

For a moment she hesitated. She didn't want to be forward. Then she told herself that they were colleagues who worked together, that he had tried to make her welcome at the clinic. No, he had done more than make her welcome.

She felt that there was something growing between them—she didn't know what but both of them were very cautious. So now she wanted to talk to him. Before she could change her mind, she walked over.

'I'm so glad you came,' she said. 'This is a good cause. Do you want to come and join us?'

He hadn't seen her approach him, he turned as she spoke. He smiled, but not in the reserved way he usually smiled at her. Instead, she saw the flare of interest in his eyes as he looked at her.

She was wearing a wine-red halter-necked dress. Perhaps it was a bit revealing but, then, a girl didn't want to spend all her life in a midwife's uniform. Still, she couldn't help herself, she tugged at the top of the dress. And that, she supposed, made it more noticeable.

'I'd love to join you,' he said. 'And I want to say hello to Jenny anyway. To thank her for finding you for the clinic.'

Maria's cheeks warmed again.

He kissed Jenny on the cheek, shook hands with Mike, Jenny's husband. Jenny said, 'It's great to see you here, Tom. You don't get out often enough.'

'I was ordered here by my new midwife. She said I had to come so I did. Jenny, it's good to see you walking so well.'

'If you've got help from your friends and your husband, you can get over anything,' Jenny said. 'When are we going to see you?'

There was a great drum roll, ending in a blasting brass chord that echoed and seemed to go on for ever. Time to start dancing again. The DJ shouted, 'Sorry for you younger people, but we need something for the oldies—a waltz. And I want a special couple to lead it—Mike and Jenny!'

There was another drum roll but this one was almost drowned by the applause. Maria watched as Mike offered Jenny his hand and she haltingly accompanied him onto the floor. Then the music started and they danced.

'Now, that is really something good to see,' Tom said to Maria.

She nodded. 'It is. I could cry but that's something I never do.'

Jenny and Mike had circled the floor twice and now other couples were joining them. 'Would you like to dance?' Tom asked hesitantly. 'I haven't danced for over four years but I'm willing to try if you are.'

'I'm not expert either. But I'd love to dance with you.' She offered him her hand and he led her onto the floor.

They were dancing. He had his arm round her waist, his fingers resting on her bare skin. Their bodies were touching and when he stepped forward his thigh pressed against hers. She had forgotten just how intimate dancing could be. For a while she was content that he didn't speak, she needed to deal with violently conflicting emotions in her breast.

She was enjoying this too much! Being held by Tom, feeling the strength in his fingers and arms, feeling the movement of his body next to hers, feeling the warmth of his breath on her face. She was enjoying it far too much! But for a while it was good to dream.

She saw that they were attracting quite a few

glances and realised that they were a noticeable couple. Perhaps her wine-coloured dress went well with his blond hair. Mischievously, she said, 'You should go out more often, a lot of people are looking at you. Every woman here envies you your blond hair.'

He thought for a moment and then said, 'If anyone is looking then I suspect they're looking at you.' He went on cheerfully, 'You know, my hair's even longer than yours. Perhaps that's why people are looking at us.'

'I used to have it longer. I prefer it short now, this style is more efficient.' She couldn't help it if her voice was curt. She didn't want to talk about why she had short hair.

The waltz ended and to more applause Mike and Jenny left the floor. The DJ announced that he would be playing something a bit more lively. Tom raised his eyebrows and she shook her head. That wasn't for her, and so they went back to their small group.

There was a lot of news to catch up on, a lot of people to see, and she lost track of Tom for a moment. He also had people to talk to. Then he came up beside her, took her wrist and gently drew her to one side. She liked it when he touched her.

'I want to stay with you, he said, 'but I really must go. I've just had a phone call—James has rather a bad headache and I want to go to check up on him. I'm sorry to leave, Maria.'

'I'm sorry you're going, too,' she said, then wondered if that was a bit too frank. 'But we'll see each other on Monday morning. At work.'

'That thought will help me through the weekend,' he said. And then he was gone.

Maria pondered. Just what had he meant by that last remark?

While she was thinking, Jenny came up to her. 'My leg's aching a bit,' she said. 'Let's go and sit down for a while. We'll talk, just you and me.'

She led Maria to a table in a quiet corner, somewhere where they wouldn't be disturbed. 'Just how well are you getting on with Tom Ramsey?' Jenny asked.

'He's a good man to work with. Very calm. A bit reserved, but I like that. Do you know him well?'

Jenny shook her head. 'Not really well. Like you say, he can be a bit reserved. I know he was born locally but he trained and worked in London. He was happily married, looking forward to the birth of his first child. And then his wife died.'

'But his son survived.'

Jenny nodded. 'Lord knows how he coped. Anyway, he took a job up here a year ago. His mother lives nearby and she helps him look after the child. He devotes his life to James. Mike says he's a brilliant doctor but he seems to avoid all social life.' She looked at Maria curiously. 'That leads us to another question. How come you managed to persuade him to come here?'

'I just suggested it to him,' Maria protested. 'We didn't even come together and he's certainly left without me.'

'I don't think he wanted to. I saw how he was looking at you. Earlier on he was asking about you. He seemed a bit more curious that one colleague asking about another, but he hid it very well. Are you interested in him?'

'I could be,' Maria said with unusual frankness. 'In fact, yes, I am. But I'm frightened. And he's got James, and every time I look at James my feelings get all scrambled up. There was my James and now this one, and they're so much alike and yet they're different and…' Her voice trailed away.

'Over the past four years you've built a shell around yourself,' Jenny said. 'Is Tom Ramsey starting to crack that shell?'

'He might be,' Maria said after a while.

Maria enjoyed the ante-natal clinic. First she ran a relaxation class and then saw the mums-to-be individually as the others drank tea and gossiped. She knew that a lot of friendships were formed at these classes. The people were neighbours, saw a lot of each other.

They formed an unofficial support group for each other. At the moment all was going well for most of them, but those who were having problems could ease things by talking through them.

Maria was just writing up the notes on the last patient when there was a phone call from Molly. 'I've got a late arrival who'd like to see you. She hasn't an appointment but do you think that you could squeeze her in?'

Maria could tell by Molly's controlled tone that the person in question was listening in to the phone call.

And that Molly felt that she should be seen. 'Send her along to get a cup of tea,' she said. 'I'll see her after I've finished with this patient.'

'Lady's name is Tracy McGee,' Molly said and rang off.

Maria finished with her current patient, smiled at her and said that all was well. Then she looked for the file on Tracy McGee. Tracy had missed her last three appointments. And lightly, in pencil, on the front of the file was written, 'Partner is no good. Drug abuse?'

Maria sighed. It wasn't an unusual thing to do, to pencil in ideas or suspicions on the front of a file. There were things that you needed to know but did not want to be written in a file that might be kept indefinitely. A pencilled comment was easy to rub out.

She went to look for Tracy but there was no one new drinking tea with the other mothers. So she looked out into the corridor and there she found her new patient.

Tracy was young, with bright purple hair. She had studs in her ears, her nose, her lower lip. She was wearing a long, khaki ex-army-style coat. And she had a disgruntled expression.

'Hi, I'm your midwife, Maria Wyatt,' Maria said. 'Didn't you want a cup of tea or coffee?'

'I don't want to mix with that lot! They'll only look down their noses at me.'

'They're only mums-to-be like you,' Maria said mildly. 'But if you want to sit in my office, I'll fetch you a cup.'

'All right, then.'

So Maria fetched the black coffee with four sugars that had been asked for and then set to examine her most difficult patient so far.

Tracy was not in good shape. She was stick-thin, obviously undernourished. Maria managed to drag out of her that she lived mostly on chips and curries. 'Plenty of milk?' Maria asked. 'You need the calcium for the baby's bones and your teeth.'

'I don't like milk!'

Tracy's pulse and heartbeat were within acceptable levels—just. But her BP was slightly too high at 135 over 95. The baby was small, its heartbeat not very strong.

'Where do you live, Tracy?'

'I live with me fella. We've got this place in the flats. It's a bit of a mess—but he's all I've got.'

'Are your parents nearby?'

'Mum's dead. Last I heard of him, Dad was in prison.'

It had to be asked. 'What drugs do you do?'

Tracy shrugged. 'You know, the usual. Whatever he can get me. Coke once or twice. But mostly weed. I need some stuff to get me through life, don't I?'

'By weed, you mean cannabis?'

Tracy looked at her with a bit of a smile. 'Yes, I mean cannabis,' she said. 'Haven't heard it called that since I went to this talk at school.'

'You know that drugs could harm the baby,' Maria said. 'I'm not saying that they will, but they could. May I refer you to a specialist clinic? They'll look after you, put you on a programme of drugs that—'

'I'm not going to any poxy specialist clinic.'

Maria sighed. But she knew that she had no powers, all she could do was try to persuade. 'I'm not very happy about both you or the baby,' she said. 'You're undernourished and the baby isn't all that strong. I think you ought to go into hospital for a few days. You both need care and attention and—'

'I'm not going to hospital. And I'm going to have this baby at home. Get it clear, I'm not going to hospital and that is certain.' And no amount of argument or persuasion by Maria could make her change her mind.

'Is this flat you share with your…fella a good place to have a baby?'

'It's the best I can hope for. And he tries to look after me. He's all I've got.'

'So how can I help you, Tracy?'

And for the first time Tracy lowered her guard. 'I just want to know what I have to do,' she said. 'I'm…scared.'

So Maria gave her the best advice she could. She talked about suitable lifestyles, suitable diets, what Tracy had to do to ensure a safe delivery of her child. And Tracy sat there and listened. But Maria could tell by her bewildered expression that she wasn't taking much of it in.

Maria sighed when her patient had left. She knew she had done all she could—but she suspected that Tracy would largely ignore her advice.

She didn't need to consult Tom. But he had said for her to drop in anytime she needed to chat about something—so she would. She poked her head round his half-open door. 'Got a couple of minutes for a casual chat about someone?' she asked. 'It doesn't matter if you haven't.'

He looked up. 'There's always time for my favourite and only midwife,' he said. 'Though I suspect it won't be casual. Do you want a cup of better-class coffee?'

'I feel as if I need one.'

He poured her a coffee, waved her to one of the comfortable chairs by the low table and came to sit opposite her. 'Business first,' he said, 'and then we can chat. Let me guess. A young lady with large quantities of ironwork in her face. I saw her talking to Molly.'

'The very same. Name Tracy McGee, age eighteen, pregnant—about thirty weeks. She's trying to be hard and yet she's scared and I feel sorry for her.'

Tom nodded. 'Give me the full story.'

So she went over Tracy's life and her fears for the future. And then asked the question that had been troubling her. 'So what can I do?'

Tom sighed and stared at the ceiling. Then he said, 'One of the hardest things a midwife or a doctor or a nurse has to do is to sit and watch while good, life-saving advice is ignored. Sometimes I think people are so stupid that they have a death wish. The answer to your question is that, yes, Tracy is endangering her health and probably the life of herself and her baby. But in the eyes of the law she is an adult. She can make her own decisions. You could inform Social

Services, it would be a good idea. But if Tracy doesn't want to see a social worker, she doesn't have to. All you can do is indicate what is best and try to persuade. It's a hard lesson but it's the right one. And I know it hurts you. It has hurt me, and so it should. But…there is nothing you can do.'

'What about the baby? What chance has the poor little mite got?'

'You know the answer to that. The minute he or she is born, we can take action—but only if it's necessary.'

Now it was her time to sigh. 'I did know that,' she said. 'I guess I just needed reminding of it. Now, serious talk over. Did you enjoy the party on Saturday? I was sorry you had to go home.'

He hesitated. 'I did enjoy the party and I was sorry myself that I had to go home. I would have liked to stay.' He grinned. 'And I saw a new Maria Wyatt.'

She decided to ignore his comment. Instead, she said, 'You should get out more often.' Then she thought that that was silly, her telling someone to get out more. How often did she go out?

He looked at her shrewdly, with the small, knowing smile that she had seen before, and she wondered if she had made a mistake. 'A good idea,' he told her. 'What are you doing next Saturday? Would you like to spend it with me?'

This shocked her, she had not expected it. And she had also not expected the instant feeling of hope and excitement it gave her. She wanted to spend time with him, to get to know him. But… 'Just you?' she asked.

'Just me. James is away with his grandmother for the weekend. For a while I'm fancy-free.'

Fancy-free, she thought. She'd never met a man who was less fancy-free. 'What would we be doing?' she asked cautiously.

'I'd like it to be a surprise. It's partly work but I think you will enjoy yourself. Why not take me on trust?'

She grinned. 'Why should I trust you?'

He grinned back. 'You think too much, Maria. I've seen you doing it. You're over-cautious. Wouldn't you like to spend some time with me?'

Well, yes, she would, she thought. But things were still a bit complicated. There was James. But it was only one day... 'All right,' she said, 'since it's work, I'd like to go. Now, I've got work of my own I'd better get on with. Thanks for the coffee.' She left the room quickly.

In fact, she had no work that was really pressing, she just needed a few minutes to herself to think. She scurried to her own little treatment room, sat behind her desk, closed her eyes and tried to relax. Had she just made a big, big mistake?

Yes, she did want to go out with Tom. Not only was he one of the most handsome men she had ever met, he was also kind and thoughtful and... She had to admit it to herself. Every time they met her body responded to him. She could feel the hairs on the back of her neck come erect, her breasts felt taut, she knew her face was warm, even slightly flushed. He excited her. No man before had ever made her feel this way. And he seemed to…like her?

But there was James, he was the problem. Then she felt ashamed of herself. How could she call a likeable, four-year-old boy, who had lost his mother, a problem? If there was a problem, it was with her. She would have to learn to cope with it. Perhaps Tom would help her.

CHAPTER THREE

SHE wore a smart trouser suit in a dark amber shade, with a heavy coat over it as it was winter. Maria had told Tom she needed to know what kind of clothes to wear. He had looked surprised at that and had told her that they were going up onto the moors, but afterwards they might have a meal. So this was the outfit she had chosen. She felt well in it.

'I'll pick you up at the nurses' home,' he had told her.

That had been a bit of a surprise. 'You know that'll be taken as a bit of a statement,' she told him. 'The two of us, off together, not on hospital business but obviously on a social trip. We'll be seen, there'll be gossip, questions asked.'

'If you can put up with it, so can I.'

Well, so be it. She felt that she was starting down a road and didn't know her destination. She was frightened but it was a road she intended to follow. At least, for a while.

When he picked her up he was dressed smartly, too—a dark sports jacket, shirt and tie. The darkness of his clothes contrasted with the brightness of his hair, and she gasped at the effect it had on her. And then, as he handed her into the car, two nurses from the home came down the path and smiled at them. Well, that was that. Things were in the open.

He took her out of town, up onto the moors. And after a while he said, 'I've worked with you but I want to know what the real Maria is like.'

'The real Maria is the one you work with. It's what I am. What I'm best at is being a midwife.'

'I wonder…' he said.

She decided to go on the attack. 'For that matter, I'd like to know the real Dr Ramsey. You know you've got the reputation for being a bit of a recluse. Being a recluse must be hard for a doctor.'

'Difficult,' he agreed. 'But somehow I manage.' He wasn't going to say any more.

'I told you about my son,' she said after a while, 'and it was difficult. Now I want you know something about you. It's only fair.' She swallowed, wondering how he would take what she was going to say. 'Tell me about your wife.'

He was driving, he had to look ahead. But she thought that he might at least have looked sideways, glanced at her. But there was no such movement. His face remained in profile, unsmiling and as still as stone.

Eventually he said, 'She died an hour after James was born,' he said. 'Amniotic embolism. There was nothing anyone could do.'

'I've heard about it, read about it,' Maria faltered. 'It's supposed to be very rare and very dangerous.'

'It's both those things.' He said nothing more.

Two people, she thought. They liked each other but

neither was willing to let their guard down. She looked at the snow-streaked moors outside the car. 'Where are we going?' she asked.

He paused before answering and she sensed that he was choosing his words carefully. Then he said, 'There's money available for the clinic but it has to be spent at once. It's to be spent on toys and games for young children. Not your neonates, but the children we have aged between about three and eight. June Roberts should do it, she's in charge of the crèche. She can't come, she's got a family wedding. She suggested you. I've not much idea, I'm an Obs and Gynae man. But you seem to know quite a bit about children.'

'I've told you, you know why. I'm fine with babies, I love them. But anything to do with young children…they remind me, and it hurts.'

Tom remained calm. 'We'll soon be there,' he said. 'Just have one quick look, then if you don't want to look around there'll be a waiting room and I'll do the best I can. I'm sure I can get advice. Don't worry about it.'

And that was that. She looked at him suspiciously. He had given in far too easily.

They drove through a little town high on the moors. On the outskirts they found a big building that had obviously once been a mill, now it had a large sign saying ST FILLAN'S WORKSHOPS. Maria was curious. 'Why come all this way when there are places you can buy toys in town?' she asked.

'It's my responsibility to spend the money. So I chose where I want to spend it.' He drove into the courtyard of the building, parked in one of the visitors' slots. He came round to open Maria's door and rather reluctantly she got out of the car.

A figure came towards them, short, heavily built, dressed in a brown overall. He had a great smile. 'Good morning, madam and sir. I'm Paul. I will take you to see Mr Constance.'

Tom offered his hand. So did Maria. 'Thank you, Paul,' Tom said. 'I am Dr Ramsey and this is Miss Wyatt. Is this a good place to leave our car?'

'It's a good place,' Paul said. 'It's very cold today, isn't it?'

'It's very cold,' said Maria.

Paul was about twenty, and had Down's syndrome. Maria warmed to his smile at once.

They were taken down a dark corridor and Paul knocked on an already open door. He said, 'Mr Constance, it's Dr Ramsey and…and a lady.' Tom and Maria were shown into a cluttered office.

Mr Constance was a big, smiling man. He shook hands with them, said he was pleased to see them, then added, 'Now I've got work to do. So I'm going to ask Paul here to take you round and introduce you to people. See you later for coffee, eh?'

'Fine,' said Tom. 'Paul, I want to look at toys for children. We'd like to buy some.' Then he turned. 'Would you like to wait for me or come around with us, Miss Wyatt?'

'I'd love to come round with you.'

Paul beamed at them both. 'This way, please,' he said.

Paul proudly took them on a tour of the working area. Most of the workers in the workshop had Down's syndrome, all were working hard. It was a happy place, Tom and Maria were greeted by smiling faces and handshakes.

Maria felt pleased that she had come in rather than staying in the waiting room. After the tour of the working area Paul took them to the showroom. The workshop was a toy wholesaler as well as a toy producer, there was a very good selection there. 'I've got a few ideas,' Tom said to her. 'Largely because I know what James likes. But I don't know what little girls like and I don't know what older boys like.'

'Just use your imagination. Remember that a toy isn't going to be just looked at and played with. It's going to be thrown, dropped, sat on, kicked and scratched. It's got to be built like a tank. And it's got to be safe.'

He had picked up a wooden fort, was inspecting it with the intent expression of boys of any age.

'That's no good at all,' she told him, cheerfully cruel. 'See, it's held together with nails—panel pins. Pull off one side and you've got half a dozen spikes for kids to cut themselves on.'

'You seem to know what you're talking about.'

'Just common sense,' she told him.

In fact, she very much enjoyed looking around. If, for a while, Tom could be a little boy with his fort, then she could be a little girl with a collection of dolls. And it was fun being with him. They played, conferred, selected, noted items on the order forms that

Paul had given them. To her surprise she realised that she was enjoying herself.

Then she came to a small display cabinet. There in the centre was a wooden train, painted in black and scarlet. She recognised it at once. She stopped, her face rigid with shock. Vaguely, she was aware that Tom was speaking to her, but she had no idea what he was saying.

'Are you all right, Maria? It's warm in here. Do you want to sit down? Would you like a glass of water?'

Now she could hear him properly. He sounded concerned.

'I'm all right,' she muttered. 'Just not seen him…that for a while.'

'What? The toy train?'

'Rory, the red train,' she said. 'I bought one for James's second birthday and he loved it at once. He kept it by him always. When he was… When he was ill, he used to keep it by him in his cot.'

He took her hand in his, slipped the other arm around her waist. 'It was a shock but it'll soon be over,' he said. 'I'll take you to the office and ask Mr Constance to—'

'No! We haven't finished buying the toys yet. Give me the list, I want to buy four of these little train sets.'

He looked at her uncertainly.

'They're a well-made toy that will last and bring children a lot of pleasure. I know that. So buy four.'

'I'll buy four,' he said.

He took his arm from her waist as they had to move on. But he kept hold of her hand. She liked that.

* * *

Buying toys in bulk was harder work than Maria had realised. They spent over three hours selecting what they wanted and then going through prices, specifications, delivery dates. Surprisingly, after getting over her shock, Maria quite enjoyed it. It was a change for her to deal with problems that were not to do with real human beings. Dates, costs, simple unchanging facts—they were easy to cope with. And eventually they were finished. They shook hands with Paul again and assured him that, yes, they'd had a good time. And when they went back into the courtyard it was already getting dark.

'You were a big help in there,' he told her. 'I picked the right person when I asked you to come with me. Now, I promised you a meal and we've both more than earned it. Nearby there's a restaurant that's been recommended to me—a pub really. I phoned them and reserved a table.'

'Sounds good. I must say I'm feeling hungry now.'

Just for a while she wanted to forget where they had been. But she had enjoyed herself. And it pleased her that she had been able to advise Tom.

'It's just ahead, on the brow of the hill. You know I chose St. Fillan's Workshops as supplier so I could have some time alone with you?'

'Of course you did. And being alone with you suits me, so long as there's a waiter and a meal as well.'

'An excellent combination,' he said.

The Saracen's Head was a gritstone building, obviously old. It stood just under the crest of a hill, and they were shown to a window table that gave them a view over miles of the Lancashire plain below. It was now fully dark, they could make out towns just by their lights.

They ordered their meal and Maria asked for a white wine to start with. And then she felt she could relax.

'So you're on your own for a while?' she asked Tom.

'Yes. A bachelor for a while, and it's wonderful to go out again with an attractive woman. But I'm missing James.'

'It's hard, being a single parent.'

He shrugged. 'My mother lives very close by. James dotes on his grandmother and she dotes on him. But…like you I suspect, I spend a lot of my time suggesting to people that two parents are better than one.'

'If they are the right two.' Maria picked up her glass, swirled the wine round a moment. For quite a while she'd thought about what she was now going to do. Now was the obvious time and place. But she was scared. Still… 'Tom, is it painful to talk about your wife? Talk about what she was like, what she meant to you?'

His voice was still perfectly controlled. 'Yes, it's painful. I…I think about her a lot. But I don't talk to other people about her. I don't feel the need.'

This was going to be harder than Maria had thought. But now she had started, she had to go on. Hesitantly, she said, 'When there's been a death, too often friends and family think that the best thing to do is to pretend it hasn't happened. They just don't talk about the person. That's wrong. Your wife was and is part of you. So I'd like to know about her.'

'For any particular reason?'

'I think we're getting to be friends. Isn't that enough reason? And…you got me to talk about my James. It hurt at the time but I felt a little better afterwards.'

She wondered if he was having difficulty knowing where to start. He gazed out of the window at the lights below, and his face seemed as if it was made out of the same gritstone as the inn. But then he began, in an apparently casual voice that she knew was intended to hide the emotions he was feeling.

'Her name was Jane. I know I tend to be a bit thoughtful, a bit reserved, but Jane was just the opposite. She was bubbly and outgoing. Everyone was her friend, she seemed to spread joy just by being her. The happiest years of my life where when we were married.'

'How long were you married?'

'Just four years. We had planned our baby and were so much looking forward to him—or her. All seemed to be going well with the pregnancy. It was hard being an O and G man, knowing what could go wrong, but I managed by remembering the vast number of births that went well.'

He stopped. He hadn't turned to look at her, his gaze still fixed on the darkness outside.

'And then?' she prompted gently.

'No problem at first. James was delivered. I remember how joyful we both were. Then Jane had an amniotic embolism. For some reason amniotic fluid got into her bloodstream via the placenta, and she had an allergic reaction to it. She complained of being cold, she couldn't breathe properly and she was getting increasingly anxious. By this time so was I. We had all the experts in the hospital there, but everyone knew there was nothing they could do.

'The baby was fine. But everyone there knew there was little chance of Jane surviving. She sank into a coma. I sat by her and held her hand and she died. I wanted to die with her. But I had a baby now, I had responsibilities.'

For the first time he looked at her. 'I never want to go through that hurt again.'

She could tell that he was suffering still. She wanted so much to comfort him, to reach across the table and hold him and tell him that in time the pain would pass. But, then, who was she to talk?

'Which is why you've never started another relationship?' she asked gently.

'For a long time I just didn't have time. But now it's different. I have a son to look after and I worry enough about him. I couldn't fall in love again, risk all that pain. I'm quite happy remaining detached.'

'I'm sorry I made you go through all that,' she said. 'I know how you feel.'

He shook his head thoughtfully. 'No, you were right. I suppose I spend too much time brooding to myself, never thinking about other people. Now, do I see the waiter coming our way?'

A totally different voice, a totally different expression. The time for high emotion had passed. Now they were to behave like ordinary human beings, carefully hiding their pain from themselves and the world. But she knew that she had opened a door between them. Whether it was to be a good thing or not, she didn't know.

The dinner was superb, but afterwards she couldn't remember a thing that she had eaten. Then they drove home, and he took her back to the nurses' home quite early. She was glad of that. She felt she needed time to herself, time to think.

He walked her to the door. She put her hands on his shoulders and pulled him to her, quickly kissed him. 'Thank you for a lovely day. And this is a good-night kiss, nothing more,' she said.

'Nothing more,' he said slowly. He slid his hands around her waist, held her loosely. She knew she could escape his grip any time she wanted. But she didn't want to. She hadn't really wanted this, but now she wouldn't change anything.

She looked up at him. It was dark, but she could just make out his expression in the lights from the home. He looked perplexed, as if he was trying to work something out.

'You're gorgeous-looking,' he said. 'And you're clever and kind and generally fun to be with. I feel at home with you. And I get a thrill from just holding your hand, and feelings that I thought were dead are reminding me of what I've been missing.'

Then he pulled her to him and kissed her.

She knew she could escape from his arms, could

stop him. Perhaps it might be the best thing to do, she felt she was being taken somewhere new, that the certainties of her life might be upset. But she didn't care.

One hand caressed the back of her neck, the other was around her waist, easing her towards him. She could feel the firmness of his body, was happy at the way her own body moulded into his. They fitted so well together! At first his lips were gentle but as he felt her response they grew bolder, touching, tasting, exploring. Around her the world disappeared. All she knew was that she was here with this man, that he was kissing her and she would like to do it for ever.

And then he stopped. She moaned softly. Why had he stopped? But a cold, cautious part of her mind suggested that it was perhaps best if they stopped before things progressed too far.

'Was this a good idea?' he asked her.

'Perhaps not. It's started something that I'm frightened of.'

'So are you sorry?'

No need to think about the answer. 'No,' she said. 'Are you?'

'Who could be sorry after that? I couldn't. But what now? How will I greet you on Monday morning after this?'

'We'll work something out,' she said, and fled.

In her room she undressed, showered, made herself a cup of cocoa. Then she sat on her bed in her dressing-gown. She ought to think, decide what to do about Tom, consider how she felt. Then she decided not to. For once in her life she'd let things fall as they would.

She'd spent too much of her life thinking and worrying. And then she smiled at a memory. Being kissed by Tom had been fantastic! She wanted it to happen again.

On Monday morning she found that one problem had been solved. No need to worry how to greet Tom—he wasn't there. 'He'll be away all week,' Molly explained. 'Apparently he's been borrowed by a hospital somewhere near Sheffield. They've had some kind of a bug that has laid low all the O and G doctors. But he'll be back on Friday.'

'Right,' said Maria. She felt a bit let down. Saturday night had started something that she felt ought to be resolved. She wanted to know what he felt. For that matter, she wanted to know what she herself felt.

In the middle of the morning her phone rang. Casually she stretched out a hand—then caught her breath as a familiar voice asked, 'And how's my favourite midwife?'

'Your favourite midwife is missing you.' It slipped out before she could gather her wits.

She heard him sigh. 'I'm sorry. And I'm missing you. But there was nothing I could do, I'm afraid. This job just has to be done.'

'When are you coming back?'

'On Friday. Remember we're both going to that community hall meeting? I'm going to be in time for that. See you there?'

'I'll be there. Tom, what happened on Saturday

night. Perhaps we need to talk about it—or was it just a friendly goodnight kiss?'

'I don't think so,' he said slowly. 'Do you want to talk now?'

'Not on the phone! If I talk to you, I need to see you. It's important.'

'I agree. We have to—'

She heard the sound of a door opening near him, overheard a voice say, 'Dr Ramsey, we need you! We have a problem!'

'See you Friday,' Maria said rapidly. 'Perhaps a few days away from each other will give us both the chance to think.' Then she rang off. She had a slight feeling of relief. And a bigger one of disappointment.

Hard work had always suited Tom. And the job he was doing at the moment was harder than most. The cases seemed to pile up, the hours he had to put in mounted to a ridiculous number. But no way could he walk away from an ill mother or baby who needed his attention. So he drank the coffee that the nurses brought him, ate sandwiches sent down from the canteen and at night collapsed into bed, to sleep instantly. He had to. He knew he'd probably be woken up.

He didn't mind. Perhaps it was good for him, just for a week. He could forget what had been his calm, ordered life at home. He could forget that someone had just moved into that life, and was causing him to do more self-searching than anyone had done for years.

But from time to time he remembered. In the middle

of a hectic session with an injured child, he'd remember Maria's lips, the smile that lit her entire face. And after a while he realised that she was acting as a talisman. When he was tired or angry, when things were going badly, he'd have a vision of her. And it made him calmer. It told him that there were good things to come, his life was going to get better.

Slowly, almost reluctantly, he came to the conclusion. Maria meant more to him than… All right, he'd think the unthinkable. She meant more to him than any woman had since Jane had died.

So what was he to do now? Could he risk love again? He had always thought not. But perhaps…

'Dr Ramsey, we're a bit concerned about Emily's BP.' A harassed-looking nurse had come in. 'If you could just have a look…'

Work again.

Late Friday afternoon. It had been a hard week. Maria was looking forward to seeing Tom again, but feeling slightly apprehensive. She had thought about him often in the past few days but had come to no conclusion whatsoever.

She was driving through the winding roads of the Landmoss estate. It had been her last call, she'd been to make a post-natal visit to Sally Chester. Little Anna was doing fine.

The arrival of a baby had changed Sally's determination to keep her house in all ways neat and tidy. She was more relaxed, more easy to talk to. There were baby clothes drying by the fire, a tiny bath was stacked by the wall. After the examination and admiration of the baby, Maria had been served with the usual tea—but this time in a mug—and an invitation to dip into the biscuit tin.

'Anna's changed my life,' Sally said. 'I didn't know just how much I needed a baby.'

'Babies do tend to make a change,' Maria said.

And Sally had a question. 'How soon is it safe and proper to have another baby?' she asked. 'I'd like one soon. And then perhaps a third. It doesn't matter, I'll be happy with what happens, but really I'd like them all to be close together. Then we will need a bigger house. Brian says we'll be able to afford it.'

Then Sally the super-planner reappeared. 'And after three children Brian will have a vasectomy.'

'It's unusual to conceive while you're breast-feeding,' Maria said. 'But in another four or five months, when you're weaning Anna, it should be possible. But, remember, two babies is hard work.'

She paused a moment and then said, with some difficulty, 'Whether Brian should have a vasectomy is not my business. But you have to remember, things… things can go wrong. You might want, or need, to have another baby.'

'We'll just see what happens,' Sally said serenely.

At present the Landmoss Residents' Association met in a wooden hut, close to the clinic. There were plans for a brick building, but so far nothing had come of them. Maria decided to park at the clinic and walk over.

The hut looked to be well maintained. It had been freshly painted, the gardens outside well kept. But Maria noticed the wire mesh over the windows. A sign of the times.

She was early. Tom hadn't arrived yet but had sent word that he was on his way back from Sheffield. There were lots of mothers, no fathers, children running round. Maria was met by Eunice Gee, a comfortable, motherly lady who obviously enjoyed being someone of importance. She invited Maria into the committee room for the inevitable cup of tea.

And after ten minutes there was the screaming of a siren outside.

Eunice sighed and settled herself in her chair. 'That's the fire alarm,' she said. 'It's always going off. It'll be a false alarm.'

'Perhaps we ought to go out anyway. As a committee member you have to set a good example.'

'All right, then. But put on your coat, it'll be cold outside.' Eunice obviously thought that setting an example was a good idea. And when they got outside, they saw everyone milling about in the car park. And smoke was coming from two windows of the hut. 'It's a real fire!' croaked an amazed Eunice.

It wasn't Maria's business but… 'Have you got a fire drill?' she asked. 'Have you got instructions on what to do?'

'We're supposed to gather over there. Where people are standing.'

'And have you got a list of everyone who was in the building?'

Now Eunice was beginning to panic. 'This was supposed to be a meeting open to anyone. I don't know who's here, who isn't.'

'We'll go around everybody now, ask them who they came with and if they can see them. There's not too many people and most seem to know each other.'

Maria had never been at a fire. But she'd worked for a firm that took fire precautions with deadly seriousness. And when training she'd had a short spell in A and E, had seen some of the dreadful results of house fires.

With Eunice, she worked her way around the crowd. Then a little girl said, 'I can't see Alice May.'

'Who's Alice May, sweetheart?'

'She came with her mum. But her mum went home and said she'd be back in an hour. Alice stayed and played with us. She had a red coat on.'

Maria took the little girl's hand, led her around the group. There was no sign of Alice May in her red coat.

'When was the last time you saw Alice?'

The little girl looked sheepish. 'We were playing hiding in the storeroom but we're not supposed to go in there. Perhaps Alice has gone home.'

'And where's the storeroom?' It was important to keep her voice casual, not to upset the little girl. But inside Maria there was a growing dread.

The storeroom was at the far end of the building. Maria looked horrified. There were no flames yet, but smoke rolled out from doors and windows. And it seemed as if a child was inside.

Maria knew it was the wrong thing to do. This was

a job for professionals, she should wait and let them take charge. But there were no professionals here yet, and the smoke seemed to be getting even thicker. 'Don't let anyone follow me,' she screamed at Eunice. Then she ran through the door of the hut into the thick, choking smoke.

Memories of a lecture came back to her. 'Smoke can be as big a killer as flames. But, remember, in a smoke-filled room, there is about a foot of clear air just above the floor. Get down there and breathe it.' Maria pulled her thick coat over her head, got on her hands and knees and crawled along the corridor.

Halfway along she heard a whoosh, and out of the corner of her eye saw flames licking through a doorway. She wouldn't be able to get back this way. She crawled on, scratching her legs and arms on debris in the corridor. She was coughing so hard she thought she might be sick. She negotiated the playroom and eventually found what she hoped was the storeroom door. She reached up to open it, rolled inside and slammed the door shut behind her. It wasn't as smoky as outside—but it was getting hot.

She called, 'Alice? Alice May? Are you there?'

There was silence for a minute, then a cupboard door opened, a little girl in a red coat peeped out and a tremulous voice said, 'I'm frightened.'

'Well, come here and we'll see if we can get you out,' Maria said. 'We'll soon be in the open air.' She hoped she wasn't too optimistic.

She opened the storeroom door a little then slammed it shut instantly. No way could she lead Alice through that—the corridor was now full of flames. What other means of escape was there? She picked up a chair, slammed it against the single window and the glass tinkled onto the floor. There was a blast of cool air. Maria poked at the shards of glass still in the frame, and then felt she could weep with horror. Fastened firmly outside was the thick mesh. With the chair she battered at it, but it wouldn't move. She leaned out to push it, felt glass cut her arm.

Then, immediately opposite her outside the window, she saw a brass helmet, a friendly face, a blue uniform. A voice said, 'Move back from the window a minute, love. And we'll have you out.'

Maria stepped back, reached for Alice and pulled the little girl to her. She heard a tearing sound and the mesh was wrenched from the window. More glass was chipped away. Maria took off her coat, threw it over the window-sill. She lifted the little girl and carefully passed her through to the waiting arms outside. A fireman took her and instantly ran with her to a distant group of spectators. Then it was her own turn. She hoisted herself upwards and wriggled through the gap, to be supported as she fell downwards.

'No one else in there?' An urgent question.

'Not in the storeroom or the playroom. And I don't think anywhere else. We checked.'

She looked around. The centre of the hut was now a mass of flames. She saw a fire engine, men playing hoses onto the fire. And running towards her was Tom. 'Maria! Are you all right?' There was panic on his face, in his voice. He caught hold of her as if to make sure that all was well.

She caught her breath. For the first time she thought about what had happened and what the consequences might have been. 'I'm fine. Just the odd cut and bruise. Have you seen Alice?'

He seemed distracted, as if the question didn't make any sense. Then he said, 'She seems to be fine, the paramedics are taking her straight to hospital. But are you all right?'

'Yes! I said I'm fine and I am.'

'Well, let's get away from here and we'll talk about it.' He put his arm round her shoulders, led her away from the now raging fire.

'Maria, I've just been told—that was a mad thing to do! You could have been killed.'

'But I wasn't.' Perhaps what might have happened suddenly struck her. She tried a joke. 'Were you frightened of losing your only midwife?'

'Maria, when I heard that you were in that…that furnace, when I thought that you could be killed, I…' He shook her, almost in anger. 'How could you do such a thing?'

She was shocked at the depth of feeling he was showing. This was Tom, calm, reserved, imperturbable Tom. And he was worried about her.

'I'm all right,' she soothed. 'The odd scratch, that's all. The fire never got near me.'

He looked at her, as if unable to believe what she was saying. 'I really do think you should go to hospital. Just for a check-up.'

'No, Tom! I'm all right. Nothing wrong with me at all. I just don't want to go into hospital. I don't like fuss.'

She saw he was calming down, but still in doubt about what to do with her. Finally he handed her some keys. 'These are the clinic keys. Walk over there and wait for me. I'm still a doctor, I've got to be certain there's nothing I can do here. But I want to be with you.'

One of the firemen was standing nearby. Seeing that Maria was about to walk away, he came over and said, 'Standing orders are that this young lady should be seen by a doctor. But as you're a doctor, I suppose that's fine. But I'll walk her across to the clinic.' To Maria he said, 'In future leave that kind of rescue to us, we're trained for it. But I suspect you saved the little girl's life.' They walked across in silence.

She went into Tom's office, found a blanket and wrapped it round herself. She sat in his chair. And then she burst into tears, something she never did. Perhaps she had saved the little girl's life. Well, that was something.

Tom came in about half an hour later, sat opposite her and took her hands in his. 'I'm not needed any more,' he said. 'The paramedics there know more than I do. No more injured but Alice's mother arrived to see the fire and promptly had hysterics. Maria, you know you ought to be checked over in hospital.'

'I'm all right. And I'm not going to hospital.' She hoped her voice was firm enough.

She could tell what he was doing. He was trying to

still the tremor in his voice, he was still terrified by what had happened—or what could have happened. But there might be a refuge in acting as a calm dispassionate doctor.

'Either you go to hospital or I examine you now.'

'Tom, I'm fine, I just need—'

'The hospital or me!'

So she followed him into the treatment room.

He checked her pulse, breathing, BP, the usual things. He listened to her chest, concerned about the possibility of smoke inhalation. Then he sighed. 'You're a lot fitter than you ought to be. Now, let's look at those cuts on your legs. Take your tights off.'

They were just scratches to her arms and legs, nothing too serious, but now feeling rather painful. He washed and dressed them, decided there was no need for suturing. Then he said, 'Physically there's no great cause for alarm. But I think that you're still shocked, you ought to be watched overnight. Is there anyone you could stay with? Is your family local?'

'No,' she said flatly. 'But I'll be all right in the nurses' home.'

'Not ideal.' He thought for a moment and then said, 'Maria, I think you should come home and stay the night at my house. I'm afraid there's only me there but—'

'I'm not worried about that,' she said. Then she considered his offer. 'I accept,' she said. 'It's very nice of you.'

'Wait here a minute then.'

He went back to his office, drank a glass of cold

water. Then he filled the basin in the corner of the room with more cold water, rubbed it over his face and neck. It was truly cold and he shivered. That was what he'd needed.

As he'd examined her he'd been aware that she might have been killed—and the very thought terrified him. For the past few days he had been working very long hours. It was necessary and he had been pleased about it. It had stopped him thinking about Maria, what his feelings were for her, what he should do about her. And now he had seen her risk her life for someone. He had been terrified.

He was strangely silent as they drove to his home and it worried her. 'Tom, are you all right? You seem a bit on edge. You're not hurt, are you? Or is anyone else hurt? You've examined me, you know I'm all right. So what's the problem?'

He thought for a while. Then he decided to be completely honest. He muttered, 'When I arrived at the hut it was on fire and they told me that you were inside. There was no way I could get to you. I thought you might be dying, or even dead already. And I knew I just couldn't stand it. I've had that kind of pain before.'

CHAPTER FOUR

HE TOOK her to a pleasant detached house in the suburbs with a large garden. Even in winter it looked well tended. Tom saw her looking. 'I employ a gardener,' he said. 'I've no time to work here myself. I just sit out in it when it's warm. Come on inside.'

He took Maria into a large living room. Although it was elegant in shape and design, and held good furniture, it still had that lived-in look that made it a home rather than a room.

Maria looked around. Instantly she saw a photograph on the mantelpiece. It was of a pretty, happy girl, smiling out at the world as if everything was fine and would always be so. Maria knew at once who it was and for a moment she felt insecure. 'Is that Jane?'

'Yes, that's Jane. I wanted James to grow up knowing he had a mother—once.'

'A good idea,' she said. 'And it reminds you of her, too.'

'I think of her every day anyway,' he said.

Maria looked around the room—the dark red curtains, the Persian rug on the polished floor, the two leather couches facing each other. It made her feel uncomfortable, even more aware of how she looked—and smelt. It was childish but she wanted this man to see her at her best. 'Tom, I shouldn't be here,' she said. 'I stink of fire and my clothes are filthy and it's all horrible. You'd better take me back to the nurses' home and I'll—'

'Upstairs for a bath,' he said. 'I'll get towels, there's shampoo, I'll find you a hair-drier and all that sort of thing. And I'll dig you out something to wear. I'll get a plastic bag and you can put all your clothes in that for now. Or do you want me to put them in the washing machine?'

'I'll do them when I get back,' she said. Somehow, the idea of Tom washing her clothes was just too intimate.

She followed him upstairs and into a panelled, dark-curtained bedroom that was obviously his. He led her into an *en suite* bathroom, fetched towels from a cupboard and from somewhere produced a lady's dressing-gown. 'My mother's,' he explained with a brief smile. 'She lives very close, often stops over. Now, will you be all right in the bath? If you want, I can redo your dressings afterwards.'

'I'll be fine,' she told him.

'Well, leave the door open just in case. I'll shout if I'm nearby.'

It was a relief to get out of the smoky clothes, to wrap them in the plastic bag he had given her. And it was good to lie there in the warm water, stirring the surface into foam from the expensive bath oil he had found for her. Though her cuts and grazes stung a bit.

Maria usually took showers. When she took a bath it was usually before or after a special event—well, she supposed this had been a special event. And usually she lay there luxuriating and thinking. Lying in a long, warm bath was the best time for reflecting. But this time she didn't want to think, to have to make decisions. She wanted events to take their own course.

She didn't know how her risking her life would affect Tom. So far he'd been half angry with her, half terrified for her. Well, at least it showed that he was concerned for her. Or was it something more?

She heard noises from the bedroom behind her, sank lower in the foam. She heard him shout, 'I've found you something to wear—an old tracksuit of mine. Not elegant, but it'll keep you warm and decent. I'll leave it on the bed.' Maria sighed. She supposed she ought to get out of the bath.

His tracksuit was big on her, but she didn't mind that. Her short hair was easy to dry. Maria took a breath, went downstairs.

He had changed, too, into chinos and a T-shirt. Like hers, his feet were bare. He offered her a glass of water. 'There's a painkiller in there, it'll help a little. And after that you can have some wine. Now, how hungry are you?'

She realised she was very hungry indeed.

'I've made a few sandwiches, sit down and dig in. Your blood sugar must be low. We'll sit here and have a quiet hour or so, and then I recommend that you go to bed. Best thing after a frightening experience like you've had.'

'Yes, Doctor,' she said with a smile. But she had to admit that the programme he had outlined was ideal. There was music playing softly in the background, the sandwiches looked good and he was pouring her a glass of white wine. For a while Maria felt at peace with the world. Tired but at peace.

'So you have no family locally to go to?' he asked after a while. 'Are they far away?'

'You could say that. They live in Florida.'

'Must be handy when you want a holiday.'

She shrugged. 'I've never been. My mother died when I was ten, after a long illness. When I was fourteen my father remarried. I never got on with my stepmother. When I was eighteen and got a job abroad, I could tell that both of them were relieved. In fact, I didn't even turn to them for help when I…' She remembered that she had already told him. 'When I got pregnant.'

'That must have been hard for a nineteen-year-old,' he said.

'I coped. I learned that the only person you could trust was yourself. Mine is an entirely different kind of family from yours.'

For a moment, she wished that wasn't true. She would have liked to have had a mother like Tom's. And a son like… She winced at the thought.

He realised that she didn't want to talk. 'Perhaps so,' he said. 'Now, more wine?'

She managed to shake her head and yawn at the same time. 'I don't think so. I'm feeling very tired.'

He was the perfect host. 'Then you'd better go to sleep. I made you up a bed in the spare room while you were in the bath. You've had a busy day.'

He took her upstairs, led her along a corridor and

opened a door into a small room with a single bed with fresh-looking bedding, books and a carafe of water by the bedhead. 'Bathroom is right next door,' he said. 'I've put out a toothbrush for you and there should be everything else that you need. I'll let you sleep in tomorrow. Goodnight, Maria.'

'Tom, you've been so good to me.' She leaned forward, gently kissed him.

She had intended it just to be a friendly goodnight kiss. But on the lips. And then, somehow, she didn't move. They remained there, only their lips touching. And after a moment she put her hands on his shoulders and closed her eyes.

He waited a moment. Then she felt his arms around her, bringing her towards him. There was such comfort in the touch of his body against hers that she wanted to stay there for ever. She didn't need to think of anything now, she was safe.

Then she felt him trying to ease her away from him, and she knew why. He was worried for her, thinking that she didn't know what she was doing. That later she would regret this.

Not true. She tightened her own grip on him, wouldn't release him. And she muttered, 'You're not to let me go now. Please, Tom, I need you.'

So for a while they stood there, happy simply to kiss. It couldn't last. She felt the growing tension in him, it matched her own feelings. Her fatigue had mysteriously disappeared, to be replaced by energy and a flaring demand in her that had to be satisfied.

Without saying anything, they moved to his bedroom and within seconds both were naked.

It was an act of desperation and of joy, an affirmation of life. There was little time for gentleness, she dragged him to her as if afraid that this chance of bliss might disappear. She was conscious only of her own frantic need for him.

She became aware that his excitement matched hers. She opened herself to him, wrapped her arms around him and held him, screamed his name as together they hurtled towards a joint climax that seemed to go on and on and on so that she was lost in a maelstrom of pure sensation.

Then, panting, still hot with passion, they lay side by side. And Maria just couldn't help it, she burst into tears. He wrapped his arms around her again, cradled her to him like a child. His voice was anguished. 'Maria, sweetheart, what is it?'

'Not your fault,' she sobbed. 'It's my fault. Being with you has been so wonderful and you couldn't have been kinder. No one's ever been so kind to me before. We've got now, and that's all important. So, please, just hold me, and soon I'll be all right.'

So he held her. And after a while she slept.

Perhaps she should have expected it, it had been such a frightening day. She had the nightmare again. There was that feeling of powerlessness, that scene of horror, the awful knowledge that there was nothing that she could do about things. As ever, she woke up panting and moaning, her body soaked with sweat. But this time it was different. There was someone in bed with her. In fact, someone who woke her before her dream came to its horrible end.

'You were crying out,' Tom said. 'You scared me. I wondered what was wrong.'

'It was a nightmare,' she said. 'Sometimes I have them. About my child. I'll be all right now I know I'm here with you. Now, hold me and I'll go back to sleep.'

Once again he wrapped his arms around her. And to her surprise, she did sleep.

She woke up first. Her hand was lying on Tom's naked chest and under it she could feel the rise and fall of his breathing. She lay there thinking, remembering the ecstasy of last night and the happiness of just being with him. She wished she could stay there, see what the day brought. But she knew that she dare not, it was all too much, too soon. She was afraid of the commitment, didn't know how she'd cope with James. It was time to climb back inside her shell. But she felt sad.

She managed to slide out of bed without waking Tom, pulled on the dressing-gown, crept downstairs in the dark and made two mugs of tea. And when she came back he was sitting up in bed, the bedside light on. She gave him his tea, sat on a chair at the end of the bed.

'You could get back into bed,' he said.

'That's too good an idea. If I got back into bed with you, I think I'd never leave.' Then she shook herself.

That was not the message she had to give. As well to be brutal from the start.

'Tom, last night was a mistake. It was all my fault. I'm sorry.'

Just for once his usual calmness deserted him and she saw hurt and surprise on his face. But she hurried on, 'It may have been a mistake but last night was wonderful. I'll never forget how…how kind you were to me. I needed comfort and you gave it to me.'

'There was more than giving comfort between us,' he said. 'And I'm not into one-night stands. I didn't think you were either.'

'It just happened,' she said.

'Things like that don't just happen, Maria,' he said gently. 'They happen because two people want them to.'

Just for a moment Maria was tempted. Perhaps they could work things out, perhaps there could be some kind of a future for them. But then she remembered the words he had just used.

'I once had a chance at happiness,' she said. 'Everything was right with my world. I had a job I liked, some prospect of promotion and my life revolved round my child. Then he was taken away from me. And I vowed that I'd never be hostage to fortune again.'

'I can understand that. Perhaps I feel the same way. This is a change from last night when we were both so happy.'

'And there's James,' she said. 'Like I said, he's a lovely little boy. But each time I see him I'm torn apart because he's not someone else. He's not my son but I can see my James in him and it tortures me.'

'In time perhaps you—'

'In time! I'm talking about now!'

Tom sighed. 'Let's have a peaceful breakfast together. Then…'

'Then will you take me home,' she said.

She told him that she'd like another bath, the smell of the smoke and the fire was still in her hair. So he went downstairs and cooked breakfast. He wasn't sure what he was going to do next—but he had a growing feeling of panic. He felt he might be about to lose something of inestimable value. But also he was afraid of reaching for it. It was possible to overreach.

Both seemed to think the time for high emotion was over. They ate breakfast together companionably and then she told him that she'd like him to take her back to the clinic as she had left her car there.

In spite of his protests she dressed again in her smoke-smelling uniform. 'I'll bathe again as soon as I get back,' she told him. 'And I'll wash these. There's no way I'm going to arrive at the nurses' home wearing your tracksuit. It would be a bit too obvious.'

She looked out of the window. 'And it's raining. No one will notice that my uniform's filthy.'

'Whatever you want. We'll go as soon as you're ready.' He wanted her to stay a while longer, but realised that she needed to get back to her own place.

And he was unsure himself of how to react. Last night they had been so close. He didn't want to lose that closeness, didn't want to scare her off by saying the wrong thing.

'I think you're a nice man,' she said as he drove her back for her car. 'We'll work well together from now on. But will you, please, do something for me? Forget what happened last night?'

'That would be impossible. But I'll do what I can not to upset you,' he said. He thought that was suitably inconclusive.

At the clinic she kissed him quickly on the cheek and then ran through the rain to her own car. He waited until it was out of sight, then sighed.

Soon Tom was back home. He went to his bedroom. It smelt, ever so slightly, of her. He made the bed, lay on it and thought. His thoughts got him nowhere.

Maria was like no other woman he had ever met. Well, not since Jane. He had to add that. Maria's face, body, voice all were lovely. More than that, she was good to be with. He couldn't quite pinpoint it, there was some quality in her that meshed with his own personality. When they worked together with a patient, they could almost read each other's thoughts. There was something binding them that he had never experienced before.

So what should he do? He knew he was scared of offering any woman full-time commitment. Perhaps something more relaxed, more easygoing? But he knew better than that. To offer her anything less than full-blooded commitment would be a disgrace.

Then he smiled, a grim smile. He had been thinking that all he had to do was make up his own mind. But

Maria had a mind, too. And she had just stated that their night together had been a mistake. That it would not be repeated. He knew that James was still a problem for her. When she looked at his son, she thought of her own child. It must be hard for her. What could he do?

He went downstairs, found himself at a loss. There was no James to take out, he was away with his grandmother. Usually the two of them went on some kind of an expedition at the weekend. He packed a towel and drove to the university swimming baths, tried to exercise his way to calmness. After a hard hour he climbed out, tired but not relaxed.

Back home he looked at the phone. Maria would be in her room, perhaps it would help if he phoned her. Not really. He did not know himself what he wanted to say. He just knew that he didn't want things to end, there must be some kind of future for them.

He made tea for himself, had no idea what he was eating. Perhaps study was the answer. He took down his O and G textbooks, ran through cases he might never come across. But it helped a little. For a while he was a doctor only, not having personal thoughts.

Finally he felt fatigue creeping over him. Yesterday evening had been hard, today—in its way—had been even harder. He sat in his study, poured himself a whisky and thought about Maria. Again.

What did he want of her? She was an attractive woman and he had feelings like any man. And she was good at work and good to work with. He thought over his actions of the night before. He had brought her back to his home out of genuine compassion. When he'd said that he was not into one-night stands he had been entirely truthful. So what did he want of her?

One thing was certain. He had been married, they had been the happiest days of his life and then his wife had died. Just like Maria, he had thought that he could not stand the pain of that loss again so he wasn't going to risk it. It was a conclusion that brought him no pleasure.

He wondered. Dared he try to start a new relationship? Then he decided. He would have to ask her again.

Maria was rather surprised. It was early Tuesday evening, she was sitting in her room in the nurses' home, doing nothing very much, when there was a phone call from Tom. Then she was irritated with herself for the way, when she heard his voice, that her heart beat a little faster.

'Doesn't matter if you're busy,' Tom said, 'but I could do with a bit of help. I've got to make an evening visit to a lady living on her own.'

'So you want a nurse with you?'

His voice was apologetic. 'Actually, what I need is a chaperone. This is not a medical problem, there won't even be an examination. I've prescribed HRT for this woman, who's just starting the menopause. The woman is on her own and when I've called in the past she's been just a bit…well, friendly.'

'Get away,' said Maria.

'So, if you're not doing anything else, I'd like you to come along. I'll pick you up at the nurses' home. And I'll arrange for you to have half a day off some time in lieu.'

'There's no real need for that. Give me half an hour to put my uniform back on.'

'I'll be outside.' He rang off.

It had been four days since they had slept together. She had been anxious about meeting him on Monday morning, but he had gone out of his way to make things easy for her. He had been pleasant, friendly, had asked about her minor injuries and told her that with any luck she would not have to make any statement about the fire. Things couldn't have been better.

But she felt there had been an unspoken message in his words, in his attitude. When he had passed her a mug of coffee, his fingers had seemed to touch hers slightly longer than necessary. She had caught him looking at her with an expression she hadn't quite understood. Thoughtful? Hopeful? Assessing? She just didn't know.

Of course, after the night she had spent in his bed, things could never be quite the same between them. Too much had been felt. And now, whatever there was between them had been put on hold. She suspected this situation couldn't last. And she didn't know what to do.

He picked her up in half an hour, as promised, and took her to an expensive flat. A very much made-up, carefully dressed Mrs Jennings was surprised to see two of them, and Maria saw disappointment in her eyes. 'There really was no need for you both to come,' she said to Maria.

As Tom had said, there was no need for an examination. He answered a few questions about Mrs Jennings's condition that could have been easily dealt with over the phone. Then the three of them sat in an uncomfortable silence. Both Tom and Maria refused the offer of a drink. And before they went, Maria gave the woman her card. 'Any further problems in this area, give me a ring first,' she said. 'I'll refer you to a doctor if you need it.'

Mrs Jennings realised she was beaten. 'Of course,' she said.

'I was glad you were there,' Tom said as they walked down the stairs together. 'Perhaps I was being ultra-sensitive, but it is the quickest I've ever been able to get out of that flat.'

'She's lonely,' Maria said. 'I recognise the signs.'

He sighed. 'I know,' he said. 'I've tried to suggest a few activities to her, but she doesn't appear to want to listen. I can't offer treatment for loneliness. Though sometimes I wish I could.'

'Don't we all?'

Both knew that they weren't talking about Mrs Jennings. They were talking about themselves.

He opened the car door for her. 'Isn't it a gorgeous night?' he said.

He seemed to take her back an unusual way. They weren't going straight home.

'Where are we going?' she asked.

'We're taking a detour. It'll all be made clear in a minute.' His voice sounded slightly strained, and for the first time she felt slightly uneasy. Still, he was Tom. She knew she could trust him.

He made a couple of turns and then stopped. She looked around. They were on the promenade, overlooking the river. Other cars were parked there, but some distance away. It was clear night, the moon was out, shining silver on the dark water. Across the river sparkled the lights of a refinery, and in the distance there was snow on the Welsh hills.

'After a moment's silence he said, 'It's beautiful, isn't it?'

'Very beautiful. Why did you bring me here?'

He seemed to be at a loss as to what to say next, and she felt uncomfortable. She asked, 'Did you really want me to act as chaperone with Mrs Jennings or was that just an excuse to get me where you could talk to me?'

'Yes, I did want a chaperone. Talking to you was an…an extra. I've been thinking about this for four days, Maria.'

'Thinking about us sleeping together?'

'Thinking about us making love,' he gently corrected her. 'There is a big difference.'

'That word—love,' she said. 'It frightens me. It makes me think of pain, of loss, because of my James.'

'It frightens me, too.'

From somewhere he appeared to gain strength. His voice was more assured now he had decided what he needed to say. He stretched out his hand, stroked her shoulder. It was a very small caress, but she liked it.

'Maria, I'm only going to say this once, it's the only way I can be fair to you and to myself. We've not known each other long. But there's been something growing between us, something I haven't felt for years. We go well together, don't we? You must have felt it.'

'I know what you mean,' she whispered. 'I suppose I feel it, too.'

'I think I'm starting to love you,' he said.

'You can't say that! You can't think that you're starting to love someone! You either do or you don't, there's no room for in between because—'

'All right, I love you! I've spent years avoiding emotion, not letting myself slide into any relationship because I've been there and it ended and the hurt was unendurable. Maria, I think that if we work at it, there might be something in it for both of us.'

The words seemed to echo around the inside of the car. She looked desperately through the windscreen, wished she was away there walking those distant snow-topped mountains, where she wouldn't have to think, wouldn't have to go through this new heartache, this desperate search for a decision.

'Tom, I just can't do it,' she said. 'If there was any man who could make me happy, it would be you. But there's James to consider, as well as both of us. He deserves better than I can give him. When I look at him I see a different James and it breaks my heart. Tom, we have to stop this now.'

There was silence.

She looked at him, there was just enough moonlight to outline his profile. He was sad but he was determined.

'It's your decision,' he said, 'and perhaps it's the right one, I don't know. But we'll still work together and we'll still be friends, won't we? It'll mean a lot to me.'

'We'll work together and we'll be friends,' she said. It didn't sound like much.

'I'll not ask you again, it would only lead to grief between us. Shall we go home now?'

'It might be a good idea,' she said. 'I can't think of anything more to say. Though I wish I could.'

Tom took her back to the nurses' home and watched until she disappeared inside. Then he sighed and drove towards home. So what did he do now?

He knew that they would still be able to work together. Maria was a professional, she would never let her personal feelings hinder her work. So perhaps the best option was to forget about what had happened. To carry on as doctor and midwife, smiling politely, conferring over their patients, ignoring the fact that each had a private life away from the clinic. Professionally, he didn't want to lose her, she was a great asset to the clinic.

Personally, he had made a mistake. Maria wasn't ready for what he had to offer her—perhaps he wasn't ready himself. The death of Jane had wrecked his life, he wasn't going to risk that kind of pain again. And because of Maria's rejection of him, he was in pain again. Not so much pain, perhaps. Or not so much pain now. Things could get worse.

He couldn't just stagger on from one emotional crisis to another, feeling the loss and the hurt every time.

Bleakly, he made up his mind. Maria would never be his lover again.

But he couldn't cut her out of his life completely. She had said that she quite liked James, perhaps he could gently bring the two together, show Maria that hers was a pain that could be overcome.

It was the kind of thing you did for your friend.

CHAPTER FIVE

MOVING like a zombie, Maria undressed, showered, then lay on her bed and stared at the ceiling. Only the bedside light was left on.

She knew it was no use trying to sleep, the minute she did pictures would flick across her brain, too vivid to be ignored. The sight of her child in the hospital cot, the sympathy of the Spanish staff, the growing knowledge that all her love and care would be to no avail.

Then something odd happened. She thought of her own child—and mysteriously his face was changed. It wasn't the face she remembered so well. It was a different face—the face of Tom's James. Maria shivered—and things were back to normal. She was cautious again. Deep relationships weren't for her.

In fact, her first meeting with Tom after that was a success. It was professional.

'There's someone waiting to see you,' Molly said when Maria arrived next morning. 'Remember that girl, Tracy McGee? Apparently she's been waiting since before we opened. She looked very worried. I've put her in the waiting room and given her a cup of tea. And I found her a sandwich.'

'You mean you gave her one of your own sandwiches,' Maria guessed accurately. 'OK. Thanks, Molly, I'll go and get her now.'

The clinic didn't have the staff to operate a full drop-in policy, but Maria knew that Tom wouldn't want anyone turned away if they could be helped. So she went to find Tracy.

'Maria, I think I'm losing the baby!' Tracy gasped as soon as Maria entered the waiting room. 'I'm bleeding and I shouldn't be, should I?'

'Things might not be too bad,' Maria said, trying to be kind and yet not raise any false hopes. 'Let's go to my room. I'll examine you and we'll see what can be done. Now, have you been eating properly? Feeding yourself and the baby? Getting plenty of sleep? And keeping off…other things?'

'Well, I've tried. Maria, I really want this baby, I don't want to lose it.'

This was a totally different Tracy from the cool, apparently hard girl Maria had examined before.

The examination was soon over. Tracy was still under-nourished and her BP was still too high. The baby was still small. And Tracy was spotting. Not losing a vast amount of blood, not a full haemorrhage, but enough to cause concern.

'You're lucky, the doctor's in today,' Maria said.' Now, don't argue, you need to see him. He'll give you a scan, we want to make sure your baby's still OK. And I'll be with him.'

'Will I be all right, then?'

'Whatever the result of the scan, you need bed rest.

The doctor may want you to go to hospital for an overnight stay.'

'I'm not going to the hospital!'

'Tracy, for the sake of your baby, you may have to.'

Maria reached for the phone. This would get the first meeting with Tom over quite easily. She put on her professional voice. 'Dr Ramsey? If you're free, I have a patient here I'd like you to look at. I think she might need a scan.'

'I'll be there at once.' Was it her imagination or was there relief in his voice, too?

He arrived in her room almost at once, looking every inch the professional in his glistening white coat. Tracy looked at him, obviously nor knowing whether to be fearful or aggressive. But Tom won her over almost at once.

'Tracy, the one thing men can't do is have babies. That's why I get a great kick out of helping women to do just that. Are you looking forward to having your baby?'

'Of course I am!'

'And a little bit nervous?'

Tracy looked at him cautiously. 'Wouldn't you be nervous?'

'I'd be terrified,' Tom said cheerfully. 'And I'd be glad of help.' He picked up Maria's notes, looked at them briefly. 'Now, I know you've been over all this with Midwife Wyatt here, but if you can be bothered I'd like you to tell me exactly how long this has been going on. Then I'll just have a quick squint at your baby through the scanner and we'll see where we go from there.'

By now Tracy was calmer. She chatted away quite casually to Tom, telling him something of the flat she shared with her partner, about how she'd like to get married but he didn't see the point.

'Is your partner looking forward to being a father?' Tom asked.

This time Tracy scowled. 'He just wants his own easy life,' she said.

But she cheered up when Tom explained what he was going to do and after the porter had wheeled in the portable machine, she allowed herself to be scanned.

'Baby's not very big and the heart rate is just about all right,' said Tom. 'But that's at the moment. Tracy, you came here because you were spotting. This is not necessarily serious but it can lead to worse things. You've just got to have bed rest and monitoring at regular intervals. I'm going to phone the hospital and arrange it. Perhaps after a night or two you'll be discharged.'

'I'm not going to any hospital! My mam died there.'

If you don't go to hospital,' Tom said, 'your baby could die.'

Maria winced, and looked from Tom to Tracy. She knew that Tom had spoken so bluntly on purpose. It wasn't like him but he wanted, needed to shock Tracy. And he had succeeded. Tracy went white and licked her lips.

'You think so?' she whispered.

OFFICIAL OPINION POLL

ANSWER 3 QUESTIONS AND WE'LL SEND YOU 4 FREE BOOKS AND A FREE GIFT!

0074823

FREE GIFT CLAIM # 3953

YOUR OPINION COUNTS!

Please tick TRUE or FALSE below to express your opinion about the following statements:

Q1 Do you believe in "true love"?

"TRUE LOVE HAPPENS ONLY ONCE IN A LIFETIME."

❍ TRUE
❍ FALSE

Q2 Do you think marriage has any value in today's world?

"YOU CAN BE TOTALLY COMMITTED TO SOMEONE WITHOUT BEING MARRIED."

❍ TRUE
❍ FALSE

Q3 What kind of books do you enjoy?

"A GREAT NOVEL MUST HAVE A HAPPY ENDING."

❍ TRUE
❍ FALSE

YES, I have scratched the area below.

Please send me the **4 FREE BOOKS** and **FREE GIFT** for which I qualify. I understand I am under no obligation to purchase any books, as explained on the back of this card.

M5KI

Mrs/Miss/Ms/Mr Initials

BLOCK CAPITALS PLEASE

Surname

Address

Postcode

Offer valid in the U.K. only and is not available to current Reader Service subscribers to this series. Overseas and Eire please write for details. We reserve the right to refuse an application and applicants must be aged 18 years or over. Offer expires 28th February 2006. Terms and prices subject to change without notice. As a result of this application you may receive further offers from carefully selected companies. If you do not wish to share in this opportunity, please write to the Data Manager at PO Box 676, Richmond, TW9 1WU. Only one application per household.

Visit us online at www.millsandboon.co.uk

'Your baby stands the best chance if you go to hospital now. I can't force you to go, but I strongly recommend it. And Midwife Wyatt here feels the same.'

'You bet I do,' said Maria.

'All right, then, I'll go to hospital. Just for a couple of days.'

'I know you don't want to go by ambulance, so Midwife Wyatt here might take you in her car.'

'Right, then,' said Maria. 'If you phone the hospital, I'll get Tracy here prepared. All right, Tracy?'

'I'm relying on you two,' said Tracy.

'Late tomorrow afternoon,' Tom said next day, 'I've got a meeting at hospital that I daren't miss. Could you stay behind here at the clinic for a while? It's just that there's to be a delivery of toys from St Fillan's Workshops. And I know that Paul and a couple of his friends are coming in the van, and they'd be delighted to see you.'

'And I'd love to see Paul again,' she said. 'I'll happily wait.'

She was very pleased to see Paul again. Together they opened the boxes and checked them. Paul demonstrated how some of the toys worked. Then she showed him the playrooms and the rest room and her treatment room. And after that they had the tea and biscuits she had brought in.

'You will come and see us again, won't you?' Paul asked her as they left.

'Of course I'll come to see you. I'm already looking forward to it. And Dr Ramsey will come, too.'

Maria waved back at those enthusiastically waving goodbye and then went to the staff lounge and made herself a coffee. It had been a hard, if productive day and she was tired. For a moment she could close her eyes.

'Not sleeping on the job? I must be working you too hard.'

Maria blinked and looked up to see Tom standing in the doorway. She yawned. 'Not asleep. Just resting my eyes.'

'Of course. Did the delivery go OK?'

'No problem at all. Paul was sorry you weren't here. I said you'd be certain to call in again at the workshop.'

I'd like that. Perhaps we could go together.'

'Perhaps,' she said. 'Or I might drop in on my own and—'

The phone rang. Tom was nearest and took the call. Maria frowned. The clinic was usually closed at night so people didn't ring at this time.

'Yes, you are lucky to find me here,' she heard Tom say, 'I am supposed to be off duty now and I— How serious is she?' His voice rose. 'And I'm the only doctor available? No, you can't send her off in an ambulance. I'll be there in twenty minutes. Make sure there's an anaesthetist handy and a scrub nurse and so on. And you'll have to find me a junior nurse to look after my four-year-old son, I'll be bringing him in with me. He can stay the night in one of the parents' flats...they can't all be full!'

Tom crashed down the phone. 'Emergency call-in,' he said. 'Apparently I'm the only doctor they can locate who's not working, ill or on holiday. But my mother's away for the night and I'm looking after James. He'll have to sleep at the hospital somewhere. This would happen tonight!'

Then he looked at her. 'Would you look after James for the night?'

Maria flinched. 'Tom, you know how upset I get when I have to deal with young children. And this isn't just a question of talking to him for a while, putting green face paint on. I'd have to feed him, bath him, read him a story, perhaps get up in the night if he's disturbed. Tom I don't think I could do it.'

'You've done it before. With your own child.'

'And all the time I'd be reminded of my own James. I'd see his face, half believe he was still alive!'

'I think you could manage, Maria. But, no matter, we'll work something out at the hospital. See you tomorrow.'

He was on his way to the door before she spoke. 'OK, I'll do it. I'll stay the night with James in your house. I have been there before.'

Now he seemed doubtful. 'I've talked you into this, Maria. I've made you feel guilty, I've not thought of what you—'

'You're wasting time,' she snapped. 'There's someone waiting for you at the hospital who needs your attention. Give me the keys to your house and we'll put James in my car. Then you can go.'

She could tell that it was the thought of the patient waiting for him that convinced him. 'All right. Let's do it. But if there's any emergency you're to phone me and—'

'There won't be an emergency. James and I get on very well. Let's go and tell him what's happening.'

'Right,' he said.

Maria heard Tom come in in the middle of the night. She was in James's room, there was a spare bed in there as well. She heard his car outside, and minutes later the bedroom door was quietly pushed open. She had left a nightlight on, knew that he could see that James was fine, and that she was asleep.

Of course, she wasn't asleep. But she didn't want any kind of conversation with him, she would feel too vulnerable. So she breathed like a woman asleep and after a moment the door was gently shut. Then she felt rather disappointed.

The three of them sat down to breakfast together. 'How did it go, then?' Tom asked.

'Maria read me an extra-long story,' James said. 'We had a super time, Dad. Can she come again?'

'Perhaps,' said Tom. 'If she can find the time.'

'I think I can find the time, if I'm asked,' Maria said. 'And I thoroughly enjoyed staying with you, James. It was great.' She looked at Tom as she spoke, and knew that he had received her message.

'No problems, then?' he asked, apparently casually.

'Just getting used to things I hadn't done for a while. But I remembered and then things were OK.'

'That's good. And, look, we're even twenty minutes early. James, just for once, you can go and watch a video.'

'I want to watch the pirates.' James scurried away.

She was alone with Tom now. 'So how did it go?' he asked.

She was honest. 'Very hard at first. I got nearly tearful a couple of times. But then I fell into a rhythm and I coped.'

'But not something you'd want to do every day?'

She had to be honest. 'Not quite yet. At times it was stressful.'

'At times,' he said. 'Well, that's a start. What do you think about an occasional trip out, just the three of us? Nothing heavy, just enjoying ourselves.'

'Yes,' she said after a while. 'I think I could manage that. In fact, I think I'd like it.' Then something else struck her. 'What about the case you went in to deal with? Everything go all right?'

He smiled. 'Good news. Do the right thing at the right time—a very simple thing but with great consequences. No one could quite work out what it was. But eventually we did, we treated it and the patient will survive.'

'And that makes you happy?'

'I'll bet you know how happy it makes me. Now, time for us to go to work.'

* * *

That night Tom lay in his own bed and stared into the dark. Sleep was evading him, he was thinking about Maria.

They seemed to have struck up a new, curious relationship. They were still easy with each other, enjoyed each other's company. They worked well together. And he felt that he had helped her overcome a little of the pain that she had been feeling.

Was there no chance of returning to the way things had been between them? The way he thought things might have been that glorious night when they had slept together? He guessed, not really. So it was as well to keep some distance between them. He must give up that vision of a future with her that had seemed so full of promise. He'd make do with what he had.

CHAPTER SIX

HE PEERED round her door in the middle of Monday morning. Maria was sitting at her desk, looking through the paperwork that was a vital part of every midwife's job. She thought Tom looked a little apprehensive.

'Quick question,' he said. 'You don't need to answer at once, you can think about it. There's a place in Ellesmere Port called the Blue Planet. It's a sort of wonderful aquarium. James has been talking about it for weeks, and I said I'd take him next weekend.'

'I've heard of it. It sounds a great place, you'll both enjoy it. But what's the question?'

'James wants to ask you to come, too. So I thought I'd give you warning, give you a chance to think about your answer.'

After a moment's thought, she said, 'A week ago I would have said no. I'd have been scared of going out with a little boy. But things seemed to be changing with me. I think I'd like to go.'

'Good. I'll tell him he can come down at lunchtime and ask you in person.' Tom still seemed a little ill at ease.

'Do *you* want me to come with you?' she asked.

'Very much so,' he said after a moment. 'It's the

kind of things that…friends do together. James and I will enjoy your company.'

It seemed rather a formal way of putting things, but she knew what he meant. This was not any kind of sexual advance on his part. Well, that's what she had said that she wanted.

'If he comes to see me in my lunch-break, we can have a chat,' she said. 'I'd like that.'

For a moment he looked at her in silence. 'You really would?'

'I really would like to chat to James for a while,' she said.

'Right. He'll come.' And Tom was gone.

Things had been just a bit awkward, Maria felt. But they were easing their way into their new relationship, one of closeness perhaps but with no sexual expression. And a rebel part of her mind taunted her that this was not what she wanted at all.

James did come to see her a couple of hours later, carrying a leaflet with details of the Blue Planet. They looked at it together, worked out exactly what they would like to see.

'The sharks can't get out, can they?' James asked, very seriously. ''Cos they can kill you.'

'I don't think the sharks can get out. But there's a pool here where you can dip your hands in to see what underwater creatures feel like.'

'There are no sharks in that pool?'

'No sharks in that pool,' Maria assured him.

'And Daddy says he knows a place nearby where we can go for a sandwich and a milkshake afterwards.'

'That'd be nice, too.'

So it was settled.

It was a good trip to the Blue Planet, James was entranced and Maria shared in his excitement. There was the pool to feel sea urchins and anemones and there were frogmen who fed the fish and waved at them from underwater. There was an underwater glassed-in tunnel through the centre of the vast aquarium, where they could stare at the fish and see the fish staring back at them. When the sharks came close, James clutched her hand tightly. Maria squeezed his hand back and felt a deep emotion that she just didn't want to understand. Being with James was getting better all the time.

Afterwards they went for the promised sandwich, and a milkshake for James and coffee for her and Tom. James wanted to start colouring in his newly bought book at once, but was persuaded to wait until he got home. He could hardly contain his enthusiasm.

'That was fantastic, wasn't it, Maria?' he said. 'Have you ever been to an aquarium like that before?'

'I've been to a place called Marine World,' she said. 'It's on an island called Majorca. There were no sharks but there were dolphins and they jumped out of the water. That was fantastic, too. And afterwards we went to a place called the Green World. And that was full of snakes.'

James gave a great shudder. 'I don't like snakes,' he said. 'I like sharks better now but I don't like snakes. Did you go to this place on your own?'

Maria was sitting next to Tom. Without looking at him, she felt his reaction, a stiffening of his body, a quick intake of breath. 'James, you're not eating your sandwich,' he said. 'Don't bother Maria. She wants to—'

'I did go with someone,' Maria said. 'I went with another little boy and he was called James, too. We had a great time together.'

'I'll bet you did. But I still don't like snakes.' And James turned his attention to his sandwich.

Maria lifted her chin, turned to look at Tom. She saw the concern in his eyes.

'I did go with James and I remember it being a wonderful day.'

He reached over to squeeze her hand. 'The hard thing is remembering the good times and trying to separate them from the grief that followed,' he said. 'It's something that comes, but it comes slowly.' Then he quickly released her hand.

'I'm getting there,' she said. 'I'm getting there quite quickly now.'

He took her back to the nurses' home, and she turned to kiss James before she got out of the car. Tom got out, too. It was dark now and although they stood facing each other it was hard for her to read his features. 'Have you had a good day?' he asked.

'I've had a wonderful day. I was a bit cautious at first—but James is good company and I've really enjoyed myself.'

'James is good company?' he asked, mock anger in his voice. 'What about me?'

'You're always good company. With you I know I'm with a friend.'

She reached forward and kissed him, too, kissed him quickly so he wouldn't guess what she was feeling, what she was missing. She could feel her body yearning for him but they had made their decision, there was to be nothing like that between them.

'Goodnight and thank you, Tom,' she said. But she didn't turn to go.

'Why thank me? I should thank you.'

She could have cursed herself the moment she'd said it. 'I'm thanking you because you've respected our decision,' she said. 'That we're just good friends.'

Perhaps there was a flicker of strain in his face. But his voice was calm and pleasant when he said, 'We're just good friends. Of course. What else? It's what we decided. Goodnight, Maria.' Then he turned to go.

Maria sighed. Why did she say the wrong thing so often?

Three days later Tom's mother phoned her at work. 'I'm Kate,' she said. It's James's birthday party this weekend. If you're not doing anything special, would you like to come? I gather you've been seeing a lot of him recently. You could help me run the games—and James is very fond of you.'

'I'd love to come,' Maria said, 'and I'd like to help. Have you asked Tom about inviting me?'

'I didn't ask Tom, I told him. He said that he knew James wanted you to come.'

Maria thought quickly. This could be a self-set task—could she manage? 'I've done a lot of running children's parties,' she said eventually. 'It used to be part of my job. Would you like me to come early—help with the catering and getting things ready?'

'That would be lovely but…dear, you work so hard during the week. Are you sure you want to?'

'Oh, yes, I want to,' said Maria. 'Well, I think I do.'

She arrived just after lunch on Saturday. Three hours to party time, plenty of time to get organised. Tom was there in an apron, he seemed to be a little put out by the confident way in which Kate and Maria took over the kitchen. Maria had discussed the menu with Kate, had made suggestions, had promised to bring things along. It was fun, practising skills she hadn't used in years.

At four o'clock things went badly wrong. Tom had to go into the hospital. He hadn't expected that to happen, but he was second on call, and the other senior registrar was already occupied with an operation.

'I don't want to miss James's birthday,' he complained to Maria and Kate. 'A little boy is entitled to have his father with him on his birthday.'

'Some other little boy might not have another birthday if you don't get to the hospital,' Maria tartly pointed out. 'James will miss you. But he'll still have a good time.'

'Then I'll go,' he said.

It was a good party. Long forgotten skills came back to Maria, she knew just which shy child to encourage, just which boisterous child to calm down. She knew how long a game should last, she made sure that every child won a prize, apparently through his or her own efforts. And when there was the inevitable spillage, she mopped up and reassured the embarrassed child. It was a good party and at the end she was as exhausted as the children she had entertained.

'I gather you're an expert on parties,' one of the mums said when she came to collect her child, 'and this has apparently been a really special one. I don't suppose you'd do it professionally, would you? I'd love you to organise my party, and I know no end of people who'd like you to organise theirs.'

Maria shook her head. 'It's good of you to ask, but I'm a midwife,' she said. 'Most weekends I'm just too tired to do anything but rest.'

'A pity.' The woman looked shrewdly at Maria. 'You're Dr Ramsey's midwife?'

'I work in the same clinic as him.'

'He's a lucky man, having you. I hope he realises it.'

Maria said nothing.

James had had a wonderful party but now he was exhausted. As Kate and Maria had a necessary cup of tea, he sat in front of the television, watching a video that had been one of his presents. His head started to droop.

'You go and bath him and I'll clear up in the

kitchen,' Maria said. 'No, don't fuss, I'll be quite happy doing it.'

So when Kate came back down the kitchen was clean again. 'You'd make a great wife and mother,' she said to Maria.

They had a glass of wine together. But Tom didn't come back and after a while Maria went back to the nurses' home.

As she drove she thought about what Kate had said. Obviously it was a hint—and an indication that Kate would be happy if she and Tom got…well, closer. And sadly Maria realised that she had enjoyed being almost a mother. As for being a wife, well, that was not to be thought of.

A few days later Maria rearranged her morning programme and went to the crèche to show June Roberts how to use the face paints. The morning was a tremendous success. June had brought her camera, would take pictures of the children and promised them a copy each.

Maria was applying black and gold paint to the face of a little girl, carefully turning her into a tiger. A voice behind her said, 'Oh, dear, it's a wild animal in my clinic.'

The tiger-faced Emily giggled.

Maria couldn't help it. Whenever she heard Tom's voice, and wasn't prepared for it, a thrill ran down her spine. It was half excitement, half anxiety. What did he want with her now?

He came round and crouched in front of Emily. 'Can you growl like a tiger, Emily?' he asked.

Emily could, and did.

Maria applied the last line of gold paint and said, 'You're done now. Go and look at yourself in the mirror.' And Emily ran to join the other happily shrieking children.

'You appear to be quite a success,' Tom said. 'It seems as if you're enjoying yourself.'

Maria wondered if there was a slight touch of annoyance in his voice. Certainly it had changed in tone since he had spoken to Emily. Why should he be annoyed?

'It's just for an hour,' she said. 'I'll be getting back to my real work soon.'

'I'm sure you will.' He frowned, as if something was worrying him. 'James says that you said something about a puppet show at the hospital. That you'd take him if it was all right with me.'

'Tom, I did and I'm sorry. I should have asked you first but it just slipped out. It's on Friday afternoon, on one of the children's wards. I just thought he might like it. Of course, if you've got something else planned, I—'

'I've nothing planned for him. Of course he can go. But you know I can't come. I have a clinic then.'

'I know. I'd have to take him myself.'

'That's settled, then. Thanks for what you're doing for him, Maria. He appreciates it.' And Tom left.

Maria looked after him, dismayed. James might appreciate her, but apparently Tom did not. His manner had been decidedly curt. Well, perhaps that was the best way. They had decided to be friends and colleagues, and anything that reminded them of what they had been to each other could only lead to grief. She realised that this was his way of coping with things.

But she missed the old Tom.

Tom sat at his desk and pondered.

He'd left the door of his room half-open—he always did unless he was having a private conversation. It meant he could see what was happening outside and he hoped it meant that other people could see him, know he was part of the team. It was an old saying but a good one. 'My door is always open.'

Right now, though, he was pleased for a different reason. In a minute or two he knew that Maria would walk past the door. And he would see her walk down the corridor. Just to watch her lithe, long-legged walk gave him pleasure.

He had been ready to take a chance, to offer her…he didn't know exactly what, but to him it had represented a risk. He had even used that word 'love'. And it was not a word he used idly. He had thought she had responded to him. In fact, he knew she had responded to him. No one could have faked what they had enjoyed together in his bed.

But then she had rejected him. And it had hurt. He was not going to risk hurt again.

And what had happened now? She had told him that they could not have a relationship because she was unable to cope with a small boy in her life. He had thought he had understood it. He had tried to help her out of it, acting just as a friend. He seemed to have succeeded too well.

Or had he?

Perhaps the fear of children had just been an excuse. Perhaps she had no real feelings for him.

He sighed. Perhaps things had been better before, when he had been more or less content with what he had. Maria had been a sudden magic possibility, a chance at happiness he had thought gone for good. But it was not to be. She was just a colleague.

The next week was hard for Maria. Tom seemed to get more reserved every time she saw him. If anything, he was more formal than when they had first met. His manner was professional and proper, there were none of the little jokes that they had once shared. Once she had thought there was the possibility of a relationship with him. That possibility had disappeared. Perhaps he just wasn't ready. Well, that was too bad.

And what made it worse was that she was getting more and more fond of James. He was allowed to come to her room at lunchtime. Tom came in once when they were sticking a picture up on her wall and had told James that he must be careful not to interfere with Maria's work or bother her too much. James had been crestfallen and Maria had said that she was always pleased to see him. She didn't know what to make of Tom's unyielding face.

Then one morning, before she could start her clinics, Tom asked her into his room for a quick conference.

His voice was professional, even brusque. Well, if that was the way he wanted to treat her, Maria would go along with it. 'I think we've got a problem,' he said. 'Tracy McGee.'

Maria sighed. 'I'd hoped things were going well there.'

'They were. But I've just had word from hospital—they've suddenly got worse. After a bit of initial trouble, Tracy settled in quite well. She got on with a couple of the nurses and was making progress. She'd even had a short talk with the drug liaison officer. Then after a while her partner turned up, created havoc on the ward and persuaded her to sign herself out.'

'She must be mad! I'll go round and see her.'

Tom shook his head. 'Perhaps not a good idea. The spotting had stopped. One of the nurses there thought that at last Tracy had got some idea of how to look after herself. At the moment she and her baby are probably in no immediate danger. I suspect that a call from anyone in authority would make things worse. What do you think?'

Maria's first inclination was to march straight round to Tracy's flat and demand to see her. But then… would that do Tracy and the baby any good? As Tom had suggested, it probably would make things worse.

'I suppose you're right,' she said. 'We'll just have to hope that Tracy shows some common sense.'

'True. But isn't it the hardest thing in the world to

do nothing? I'm not good at it at all. But I know that it's sometimes necessary.' She could tell that he was looking at her assessingly, wondering what to say next.

'We're not talking about Tracy now, are we?' she asked. 'We're talking about you and me.' She managed to smile, if weakly. 'Tom, we got things right. You've made me happier by showing me that I could get on with little children. Well, with James, anyway.'

'Ah. Happier but not yet happy. Have you had the nightmare again?'

'Not really. I had a dream the other day that was a bit upsetting, but nothing like how it used to be. Tom, is there something else you want to talk to me about?'

He looked uneasy. 'Well, yes. I'm due to take a week off in a week's time. My mother, James and I were going to fly out to the Med for a winter break. But I've got a sister in Australia called Amy. She's just had her first baby, a bit premature but everything is apparently going well. And my mother wants to go at once to see her. She'll miss her holiday with us.'

'Seeing her daughter, a new grandchild and a trip to Australia should make up for it,' Maria pointed out, unable to stop herself grinning.

'Quite so. I'm pleased she's going, she doesn't spend enough time just enjoying herself.'

Maria was puzzled. She was interested, but how did it affect her? Then Tom said, 'There's a room booked for her at our hotel. I wondered if you'd like to come in her place. With James and me.'

'What?' This was the last thing Maria had expected.

'Before we go any further, let me say that the holiday is in Majorca. That might hurt. But you told me you hadn't been on holiday for four years. I think you need one, even deserve one. And I thought that you might like to go with us.'

'Go with you and James to Majorca!'

'Well, why not?'

Maria tried to make sense of her reeling thoughts. 'I'm not sure how I'd feel when I got back there. That's where my little boy died. How could you ask me to go back there?'

'Maybe you'd feel better when you'd visited the island.' He thought for a moment and went on, 'Once, when I was a medical student, and young and a bit foolish, I went on a rock-climbing course. I enjoyed it and I got to be quite good at it. I got too confident and I fell. Not far. I slithered about twenty feet down a rockface. But it shocked me.'

'I'm not surprised,' Maria said. She wondered why he was telling her this.

'The instructor came over, checked me to see if there were any serious injuries. There weren't. So he told me to get straight back up the climb I'd fallen from. And I didn't want to. He told me it would be hard, but tomorrow it would be harder, and in a week it would almost be impossible. I was shaking and I was afraid, but I did the climb. And I wasn't scared any more.'

'The lesson being that you face your fears and they disappear. But there's a difference between my child's death and a non-serious accident.'

'I know. But the principle is the same. Are you going to come with us, Maria?'

She thought. Perhaps it might be a good idea. But she said, 'There is another reason for not going,' she said. 'I get on very well with James now. How do I get on with you?'

'We came to an agreement,' he said quietly. 'It's hard but I think it's working. I think visiting the island would be good for you. And I think the three of us would have a good time together.'

She sat there, bewildered. And then she thought that this aggravating man had caused her plenty of grief—but had also brought her some pleasure. 'All right, I'll come with you,' she said. 'But I insist on paying…'

He held up his hand. 'Maria, you'll make me angry! The room and flight are already paid for, the money can't be returned. And I do not try to make a profit out of my friends.'

'All right,' she said. 'But there must be something that I can do for you in return.'

'I'll think of something,' he said.

The rest of the morning was taken up with one of her post-natal clinics. Mums brought in their new babies for the last time twenty-eight days after they had given birth. Then care was handed over to the district health visitor. Seeing the babies for the last time was work that Maria loved and she always tried to allocate more time than was strictly allowed.

Miriam Allardyce brought in her baby Michael, the third baby Maria had seen that morning. She ran through the usual checks on mother and child. Mostly it was a matter of asking questions, making sure that the mother felt confident. Physically both appeared to be doing well. But then there was the usual five-minute chat, and Maria asked Miriam how she was sleeping.

'I'm not,' said Miriam. 'Michael's not a bad baby, he will go to sleep, but once I'm awake I just can't drop off again.'

Maria looked at the weary face, the lines round the eyes. 'Can't your husband help?' she asked.

'Barry does everything I ask him to, he's a wonderful man. But I just can't sleep! I've always been like this, it's always been hard for me to sleep. But now it's worse.'

'You're breast-feeding, you can't have any kind of sleeping pills. Not that I like them anyway.'

Maria pondered. 'This isn't an unusual problem,' she went on. 'All new mothers have difficulty sleeping. And some babies are much easier than others. Just for one night a week ask your husband to look after the baby, and you find a bed to yourself where you can't hear a thing. Get him to massage you—he'll probably enjoy it. If you buy some soothing oil it's lovely for relaxation. And have quiet music on at the same time. And then you can try this.'

She fumbled in a drawer, took out a CD. Miriam looked at it, surprised. 'What's that?'

'It's a relaxation CD, a sort of hypnotic combination

of music and words. It's worked for several mums I know.'

'Then I'll try it,' Miriam said hopefully.

The rest of the clinic passed quite rapidly. Maria was busy doing something she enjoyed so she wasn't able to worry about agreeing to go away with Tom. But when all her patients had gone, and she had a little time to herself, she thought about the trip. Revisiting the place where her son had first fallen ill and had eventually died might be hard. But she had listened to Tom's climbing story and could see how a visit might help her. But how would she get on with Tom?

The next day was Friday, and as she had worked late for most of the week she told Tom that she would be leaving early. It was still light when she walked into the clinic car park. She met Tom there. Obviously he had been waiting for her. He was carrying a sheaf of flowers—a beautiful bouquet in shades of mauve and blue and white

'Have a good conference,' she told him. 'And we meet as arranged a week today. Are the flowers for your mother? They're lovely.'

He smiled, shook his head. 'They're not for my mother, they're for Jane. These were her favourite colours. I'm going to throw the flowers in the sea, where I scattered her ashes. She loved the sea.'

His next words shocked her. 'I waited here to ask you. Would you like to come with me, Maria?'

'Yes,' she said, after a pause, 'very much so. If you want me to come.'

'I do want you to come.'

He drove out of the city and then turned down a narrow road that led through pine trees. They parked to the side of a bank of sand dunes, climbed over and saw the beach below them and then the great grey expanse of sea.

He chuckled. 'I checked the tide tables,' he said. 'This is high tide. At low tide we might have had to walk for a mile to get to the sea.'

'You can joke. I would have thought this was a sad occasion.'

'I want to look forward, not back. Come on. It'll get dark soon and we don't want to be marooned here.'

He took her hand and helped her slide down the side of the sand dune. And when they got to the level surface of the beach, he didn't let go. They walked hand in hand towards the sea.

They reached the edge of the water, their shoes sticking in the wet sand. He let go her hand, took the flowers from their Cellophane wrapper and threw them one by one into the sea. Maria watched them roll in the tiny waves, some landing on the sand, others sucked into the sea.

Then she looked at Tom's face. She would have expected him to be upset—angry even. But instead he appeared serene.

He threw the last flower, stuffed the packaging into his pocket. Then he took her hand again and silently gazed at the sea.

She felt she had to say something. 'Tom, I don't understand you,' she said. 'You came here to…to…I think celebrate the life you once led. You throw in the flowers, which is a lovely thing to do. And then instantly you take hold of my hand. We're man and woman Tom, that has sexual and emotional overtones. The two ideas just don't…don't fit in together.'

'"Celebrate life" is a good way of putting it,' he said. 'That's what I wanted to do. Not mourn any more. I think that period of my life is over. And if you don't understand me…well, I'm not sure I understand my motives myself. But I wanted you to come with me and I wanted to hold your hand.'

There was too much to think about, she just couldn't cope with it right now. 'That's nice,' she said. 'But it's getting dark, we'd better get back.'

It was a friendly silence between them as they walked back across the beach, up over the sand dunes. She wondered how things had changed.

CHAPTER SEVEN

JENNY was the only person she told that she was going to Majorca with Tom and James. 'How do you feel about it?' Jenny asked her.

'A bit apprehensive, I suppose. I'm still not sure why he wants me to go or why I'm going. And the place will bring back memories.'

'You'll be fine with the memories. But I think there's something else going on. He might not realise it but this trip is as much for Tom's sake as it is for yours.'

'What? He's just being kind to me.'

'He's trying to help himself as well, and he just doesn't know how. He wants to get out into the world again.'

'Perhaps,' Maria said thoughtfully. 'So where does that leave me?'

'Just what are your feelings for him? Are you in love with him?'

It was a question Maria had never dared to ask herself. But now Jenny had asked her and she had to produce some sort of an answer.

'He's a good doctor, I like working with him. He's a kind man, he's thoughtful, he's gentle. He's helped me an awful lot and—'

'He's also exceedingly good-looking,' Jenny put in

with a grin. 'I could fancy him myself if I didn't have Mike. Maria, give me an answer. Are you in love with him?'

'I think I could be. But I'm frightened. And I told him that…that there could never be anything between us.'

'Not a good idea. But it's your right, you could always change your mind. What are you going to do?'

'I don't know. For a while we seemed close, but now he seems to keep me at a distance. Perhaps he is just not ready for any kind of relationship.'

'He's ready,' Jenny said, 'whether he realises it or not.' She leaned forward, kissed Maria gently on the cheek. 'Good luck.'

It seemed a part of her past life that she fell straight back into without any doubts whatsoever. There was an airport, an excited, chattering little boy. The wait before boarding could have been irritating, but together they found things to do, things to look at. For her it was easy.

'I'm seeing a new side to you, Maria,' Tom said. 'I know you're a brilliant midwife, but you'd have been an equally good children's nurse.'

'I did years of this kind of thing and I always enjoyed it. Until…'

'You're enjoying it now. Just keep on doing it.'

So she did. It was strange, she hadn't realised just how many memories she had suppressed. As she walked around the airport with James, she remembered past times when she had set off to begin a new job. She remembered the anticipation, the excitement. The great majority of her memories had been happy—she had just shut them down. Well, now was the time to change.

Time to board. She was almost as excited as James. She hadn't been abroad, hadn't been in a plane even, for more than four years. Her heart thumped as she took her seat.

Perhaps Tom guessed at her mood. 'You're not nervous?' he asked her. 'An experienced flyer like you?'

'Sort of nervous. But I'm going to enjoy the flight.'

The plane was towed out, took its place on the runway, there was the scream of accelerating engines. Too late to change her mind now. She was on her way—to what, she wasn't quite certain.

She had put James in the window seat and as the plane banked over Palma airport in Majorca, she leaned over and pointed things out to him. 'That's Palma, the capital city. And look at all those little windmills! They help pump water from underground streams.' James was fascinated. But as they made the approach to landing she had to lean back in her seat.

Tom looked at her thoughtfully. 'Memories?' he asked.

'Things are coming back to me. You know this is the first time I've been out of England in the past four years?'

'I guessed. But a lot of your memories are good, aren't they? You were happy here?'

'Yes,' she said, as if the thought was a curious one. 'Yes, I was happy here. And I was good at my job.'

He patted her hand. 'Just don't think of applying for it again. I need you, you're the best midwife in the hospital.'

Was that all? she wondered.

There was the bump and squeal as the aircraft wheels touched down and then the roar of the braking engines. They had landed in Majorca. The place she had left, never expecting to return.

Of course, it was winter. The buildings were familiar but the climate was not. And the airport was strangely quiet. There were none of the thronging crowds, none of the shouting, over-excited children. Mostly the tourists appeared to be pensioners, taking advantage of the cheap rates for a month of comparative warmth.

Baggage retrieval was quick and they walked out to find the bus that would transport them to the hotel. And there, on the other side of the park, was the red and grey coach that belonged to the Hotel Helena where she had lived. Maria gulped. And when they were travelling in their own hotel's coach, the smiling hostess stood in a similar uniform to the one Maria had worn so many times and gave a similar speech of welcome.

'Is this unsettling?' Tom asked.

'Very. I'm finding it hard to realise that I've been away for over four years. I feel a different person.'

'It'll all be fine,' he said.

* * *

Maria hadn't realised how tired she really was. For four years she had not had a proper holiday, not one where she was cosseted, looked after, had everything done for her. At first it took some getting used to. But then Majorca worked its usual magic.

Tom had booked a good hotel, on the north coast about five miles from where she had once lived. Her room was luxurious and had a sea view. The food and service were both excellent, though there weren't too many guests there. She was very comfortable.

She loved being with James. But the difficult thing was working out what kind of a relationship she was going to have with Tom. He was polite, even friendly, of course—but in a remote kind of way. There still seemed to be a barrier between them. And it seemed odd to say goodnight to him and then meet him for breakfast some hours later.

He had been polite when he had explained that, though they had come together, if she wanted time to herself, by all means she was to take it. 'I'd rather spent my time with James and you,' she had said. 'That is, if you want me.'

He gave her a wry smile. 'We certainly want you.' Then he spoilt it by saying, 'Your local knowledge is invaluable.'

She hired a car for them, took them to places she remembered. And she came to realise that she was enjoying herself. She was relaxing. And Tom was relaxing, too.

After three days she drove them along the coast and pulled up outside a large hotel. 'I'd like to go in here for coffee,' she said. She knew her voice was high, trembling a little. There was nothing she could do about it.

Tom looked at the name of the hotel—the Hotel Helena. 'This is where you used to live,' he said. 'Are you OK?'

'I'm fine. I had some good times here, Tom, and I've come back to remind myself of them. In fact, most of what I've seen has reminded me of the good times.'

'I'm glad,' he said.

She knew he was glad. But there was still that remoteness in his voice.

They went into the lounge and had coffee, orange juice for James. There was a small further shock. One of the porters there recognised her and was very pleased to see her. They chatted for a few minutes, and Maria felt even more welcome.

Then James finished his juice and said, 'There's a smashing playground out there, Daddy. Can I go and play on the swings?'

'Not now,' Tom said, and looked at Maria.

'There's the English papers on the table,' Maria said. 'Why don't you read for a few minutes, Tom? I'll take James? I'll be all right,' she said, hoping it was true. 'Come on, James.'

Tom watched the two of them walk away, hand in hand. He couldn't work out exactly what he was feeling. He had made up his mind about Maria. She could be a friend but she wasn't for him as a lover. Just for a while he had been tempted. They had slept together and immediately she had said that their relationship was to go no further. Well, that was conclusive. But still he had asked her again, on the promenade, and that had been fruitless, too. And in the days afterwards he had wondered if she had really been interested in him. The story about being afraid of small boys now seemed a bit doubtful. She was best of friends with James.

So, he wanted no more pain from Maria. But keeping his distance was hard.

When they came back from the playground he could see that it had affected her. Her grey eyes were large, luminous with tears. 'I shouldn't have let you go,' he said. 'It upset you.'

She shook her head. 'I needed to do it and it was good for me,' she said. 'It's over now, something has ended. Now I can look forward to the rest of my life.'

'I'm glad,' he said.

He couldn't conceal the fact that he was a little jealous of her new serenity. He wished he had it himself.

As the time passed they got easier with each other. Maria had observed it before on holidays. She had seen so many holiday romances. And sometimes, she knew, they even lasted.

As a worker, not a holidaymaker, she had wondered how apparently sane people could so quickly fall in love. Now she began to understand. She took a decision, something that was hers alone.

* * *

The next evening, when they were having dinner, she said, apparently casually, 'I hope you don't mind, Tom, but I was asking and there is one kiddie rep working. She's covering all the hotels. I remember her, she's a good worker. And tomorrow, after lunch, there's a trip to a local little zoo and playground. So far there's only three takers. So I've booked James on it. I think he'll be very happy with Melanie.'

'And we can have the afternoon to ourselves?'

'That's the purpose of having kiddie reps.'

'A lot to look forward to.'

'An awful lot. I love being with James, but tomorrow for a few hours we can act like adults. That OK with you?'

'Fine,' he said. 'As usual, I shall leave the programme to you.'

She could see the speculation in his eyes.

The three had an exciting morning. They played in the playground for a while then they went to the local supermart and bought presents for Nana. They looked at the occasional yacht sailing round the promontory. Then they had a light lunch.

Melanie arrived after lunch in her minibus with the three other children. It was obvious that James was going to get on with them all, they were chatting instantly. And Melanie hugged Maria, said they had missed her. The new kiddie-rep supervisor was all right but not as good as she had been. It was nice to be wanted, Maria thought.

James was strapped in and Melanie took Tom's mobile phone number. Then they were off. Maria felt just a touch of apprehension as they waved goodbye. Not for James—he would be fine. But apprehension for herself—herself and Tom. Still, she had her plan.

Perhaps he had a plan, too. 'We've got at least three hours to ourselves now,' he said. 'Is there anything special you'd like to do?'

She chose her words carefully. 'I think we're both a bit tired,' she said. 'And we've had quite a full morning. Why don't we just relax for a couple of hours? My room has a better view than yours, we could sit and chat or read for a while.'

'All right,' he said after a while. 'That sounds fine to me.' So they went to her room. The sun was out, they were both wearing light sweaters so it was quite possible to sit outside on her little balcony. They had a wonderful view of the sea, sparkling as it never did in England.

On the balcony there were a metal table, two reclining chairs and another wicker couch. Tom sat on the couch. Maria sat by him.

And now she was nervous. She could feel her heart beating faster than it should, knew that her colour was higher. 'Wait here a minute,' she said.

At one time she had been quite an accomplished Spanish speaker. To her surprise, although she hadn't used the language for over four years, her skill had come back at once. She rang Reception, gave a quick order. Then she went back to join him.

'James is having a wonderful time,' he said, 'largely because of you. But are you having a good time?'

'I'm having a wonderful time. This is a holiday, Tom. It's time out. The usual rules don't apply. You do things on holiday that you'd never do at home.'

'Like build sand-castles?'

'And all sorts of other kinds of extreme sports,' she told him. And she met his questioning gaze.

There was a knock on the door. Maria went to open it and let in a waiter. On his tray was a bottle in a silver ice bucket and two tall slim glasses. He placed them on the balcony table, and after Maria's quiet request opened the bottle and filled the glasses. Then he was gone.

Tom looked at the bottle and glasses, looked at her. But he said nothing.

'This is Spanish champagne, but I used to love it,' Maria said. 'I haven't drunk any for the past four years. But now we can drink it together.'

She gave him a glass, took one herself. 'To the future,' she said. 'But mostly to now.' They both drank.

She had forgotten how much she liked the sharp drink. Forgotten how exciting the bubbles were. But now she remembered and it was good.

'I'm glad you're happy,' Tom said, 'because that makes me happy, too.' He smiled. 'And I like your choice of champagne. This is wonderful.'

They sat in silence and had soon finished the first glass. It seemed perfectly natural when he put his arm behind her, leaned over to kiss her. His lips tasted of champagne, sharp and tangy.

For a while she was comfortable sitting there, her arms loosely round his neck. She didn't feel the need to do anything much—not yet. It was good to sit there, to enjoy the touch of his mouth on hers and the touch of his lips on her cheeks, on her forehead. And to feel the slowly mounting sense of excitement inside her.

Finally he broke away. His arms were still around her, he held her and looked at her. She ran her hands through his thick blond hair, stared into his blue eyes. She could read excitement there but also perhaps doubt.

'I know what you're thinking,' she said. 'And it's good of you. You know what I'm offering you, and you're wondering why. That's true, isn't it?'

'Something like that,' he mumbled.

'Well, this will be a once and only occasion, with no commitment on either side. And it's because I fancied you first when I met you first, that time when we knelt together by the old man who had been knocked down. And since then I've found that you're kind and thoughtful and gentle. But right now I fancy you because you're gorgeous. And we're on holiday and the rules don't count. Are you going to take me to bed?'

He didn't answer, he kissed her again. Before he had been gentle. But now his mouth was urgent, demanding, and she thrilled at the thought of what was to come.

Both stood. He wrapped his arms around her properly, then pulled their bodies together. She could feel the muscles of his arms, back and chest, knew from the pressure on her thigh just how desperately he needed her. At least as much as she needed him.

Then he released her. 'Come inside,' he said. His

voice was thick, hoarse with excitement. The same excitement as she was feeling.

They stood by the foot of her double bed, and now she was a little nervous. What if she disappointed him? She knew she hadn't done so last time, but then they had both been filled with the excitement and terror of the fire. Now it was different.

It was magic. He knew exactly what she was thinking. 'The last time we made love,' he said to her, 'we were in a hurry. We both needed someone to share our joy in just being alive. This isn't to be like that. I want to make love to you slowly, to enjoy every blissful minute. I know you're going to make me happy and I want to make you happy, too.'

'Just being with you makes me happy,' she said. 'Do you want to undress me?'

That morning she had dressed with care. This moment was not entirely spontaneous, she had thought about it, even planned it. She wanted to please him.

First he eased her thin sweater over her head, threw it carelessly on the nearest chair. Then, button by button, he undid her shirt. He eased it out from under her waistband and pulled that off, too. Then he caught his breath as he looked at her.

It was the most expensive underwear she had ever bought. Especially for this encounter—if it ever took place. She had sneaked an hour in town yesterday, said she had some boring shopping to do. As she had slipped it on she had known it was different, it felt so soft. Bra and French knickers in the most delicate of black lace. And as she looked into Tom's now heavy-lidded eyes, she knew it had been worthwhile.

He slid his fingertips along the insides of her arms, stroked them across the swell of her breasts. She felt her nipples tauten, swell with desire. He bent, kissed her shoulders, but no more than that.

He was in no hurry. He didn't even try to unhook her bra, contenting himself with running his fingers, still very gently, across the black lace that contained her taut breasts.

One hand moved to her waistband, undid the button there and then slid down the zip. She felt her jeans slide down her legs, waited a moment and then stepped out of them. He stepped back, and she heard him sigh as he looked at her. She'd never bought French knickers before. If this was the effect they had, then she'd buy more.

Her earlier desperation had now changed. This was to be a long slow game, a symphony that could only come to a climax when the time was right. Each moment was to be enjoyed. And she was safe in the knowledge that they had all the time they needed.

It was her turn. She pulled the sweater over his head, thrust down his chinos. She marvelled at the smoothness of his skin, the muscled arms and torso. And then the sight of him fully naked, his need for her only too apparent. Maria felt the blood rush to her cheeks, felt the thrill of anticipation grow even stronger.

Now he reached behind her, dextrously undid the

clip of her bra. It tumbled forward, down her arms. She threw it to one side, and he bent his head. In turn, he took the pink tips into his mouth, kissed them and she shuddered as the roughness of his tongue made her excitement mount even further. But there was a long way to go yet.

He kissed her quickly, then reached an arm behind her legs and lifted her bodily onto the bed. She lay there, deliberately put her hands behind her head so that her breasts were outstretched, offering themselves to him. And she gloried in the excitement, the wonder, she saw in his eyes.

The bed sagged slightly as he lay beside her. He pulled her to him, kissed her until she felt her bones turn to water. There was nothing this man could not do to her.

He reached for the bottle of champagne. Carefully, he tilted the bottle so that a thin stream of liquid splashed down onto each rosebud-tipped nipple. She shivered at the coolness on her heated flesh, but smiled as she felt the bubbles erupting on her skin. Then he took each breast into his mouth, licked away the coolness, and the sensation was so exquisite that she arched her back, trying to push herself even further towards him. 'That is so good,' she moaned.

'I can taste your skin. I want to kiss you, every inch of you, all over your body. Maria, sweetheart, do you know what you're doing to me?'

'I'm doing to you what you're doing to me,' she muttered. 'Tom, this is more wonderful than anything I've ever felt.'

His head roamed her body as she lay there. He kissed the insides of her arms, the palms of her hands, her shoulders, her neck, but returned always to her breasts. And from time to time the rest of his body touched hers, and she felt the hardness, the dampness of him, and understood his growing desire.

And there was her own growing desire. This was good, this was wonderful, but surely there was more to come? 'Tom, I want…I want…' she groaned.

He knew what she meant. She felt his hand steal downwards, slide under the elastic of her knickers, gently ease them down. She wriggled, made it easy for him. And then they were naked together. Once again his head roved down her body. She felt his hands gently part her thighs, felt his cheeks on the damp curls there and then there was the warmth of his breath on her, the touch of his tongue on that most secret of places.

Again her body arched. She grasped the pillow, then flung down her arms to grip his shoulders. 'Tom, Tom, please,' she cried. 'Oh, Tom, I can't… You must… It's too much and I…' She didn't know whether she was pleading for him to stop or to continue.

He knelt above her, she looked into that dear face, now taut with passion. She put her arms around him, pulled him down to kiss him.

And then she sighed as he entered her. They were together, they were one. She knew exactly what he wanted because it was what she wanted. And both needed. For a while they were gentle together, a soft easy movement that was as natural as life itself.

It could not last. Sensation seemed to be spreading outwards from the very core of her. Something told her that this was the time, that there was more to be felt, to be enjoyed, that this was only halfway. So she opened herself to him even further, rocked with him as she felt his increased need, called out his name. And then, so wonderful that although it must have been over in seconds it seemed to last for hours, there came their joint climax. For a while the earth stopped. And then he collapsed on top of her, his chest heaving, as was hers.

'You're so good to me,' he muttered.

'And you're good to me, too,' she answered.

For a while they were happy just to lie there. Maria thought over what had happened, knew it was something she would never forget.

She thought of what she had said to him, said so definitely. *A once and only occasion with no commitment on either side.* At the time she had meant it. Only now did she realise just how much she had been fooling herself. Tom meant everything to her. But she had made it clear that this had to be a *once and only occasion.* The words echoed in her mind, she knew they would haunt her for weeks to come.

Of course, perhaps he'd ignore what she had said. But she doubted it.

There might be no future. But there would always be memories.

That night was their last at the hotel and Maria was enjoying herself. The dinner had been good, she'd shared a bottle of Spanish red with Tom, the ice cream they were eating was far richer than anything she ate in England. And a voice said, 'My goodness! It's Maria, Maria Wyatt in my hotel. They said in the Helena that you were back but I didn't believe them. Maria, it's so good to see you.'

Maria looked up, then stood. There was a tall burly man with a beaming smile. 'John Kersh! John, it's good to see you, too.' She threw her arms around him, hugged him, kissed him on the cheek.

When she released him John looked at Tom and James and smiled. 'Don't tell me you've brought your family with you,' he said. 'You were single when you left.'

'I'm still single. This is my good friend Dr Tom Ramsey and his son James.'

There was the necessary shaking of hands and Tom asked John if he'd join them. Maria noticed that Tom was hospitable—but also a little wary. He didn't quite know what to make of John, couldn't guess his relationship with her. Maria felt rather smug.

'I'd love to join you for a minute. Now, if you're having coffee, can I get you a liqueur each from the boss's special bottle? And you, young man…' he looked at James '…may I get you a special drink, too?'

'Yes, please, sir,' said the always polite James.

John raised his hand and a waiter was instantly at the table. There was a whispered order.

'John was my supervisor when I left,' Maria said

clearly to Tom. 'He helped me a lot. I couldn't have managed without him.'

'You were a star member of my staff, I had to look after you. Now, what have we here?'

The waiter had returned to the table. There was the usual pot of coffee, with the small cups. There were also three glasses and a bottle of brandy. And for James a magnificent concoction of orange juice and froth, with two plastic flowers, two bendy straws and three sparklers sticking out if it.

The coffee and brandy were poured. Maria saw Tom sip the brandy, raise his eyebrows. She sipped herself. The drink managed to be both smooth and fiery. Obviously the manager's bottle.

'So what did you do when you left us?' John asked.

'I trained to be a midwife. I work for Tom here, we look after women having babies and women with neonates.'

'I see.' Maria saw John glance at Tom, and then back to her. 'You've made yourself a home back in the UK? You wouldn't want to work out here again?'

'Probably not.'

'A pity. I'm manager now of all the firm's hotels on this side of the island. I could offer you a job. Tom, would you be willing to release her?'

'She's mine,' said Tom cheerfully.

The two men were joking, of course.

'Well, the offer's there. Maria, I almost didn't recognise you with short hair. I remember it down to your shoulders.'

Maria shrugged. 'Just a change in style,' she said.

'I had it cut as soon as I got back to England. This length is more convenient. Tell me more about this job, John.'

'We want someone to supervise kiddie reps. The person in charge would be responsible for all our hotels on the island—that's now a couple of dozen. It's a full-time job, there'll be a car and a villa provided, of course, and the pay would be generous. Very generous. And I think you'd be ideal for the job.'

Maria glanced at Tom. As ever, his face was inscrutable. Why couldn't he help her? Just a sentence or two saying that he needed her, that would do. But he said nothing. 'When would this job start?' she asked.

'At least before the beginning of the holiday season. We're flexible, we're willing to wait for the right person. If you're interested, just let me know. You could start as early or as late as you liked.'

She wasn't really interested but she said, 'I'll be in touch in a week or so to let you know.'

'No hurry,' said John.

There was a sucking noise from the table. James had just come to the end of his drink. 'That was very nice,' he said.

'I think,' Tom said, 'that you're a tired little boy. We'd better get you to bed.' He stood, offered his hand to John. 'Good to have met you,' he said. He added to Maria, 'If you'll excuse us, we'll see you over breakfast. You stay here and chat with your old friend.'

Quickly, Maria said, 'I'm tired, too. I'll be soon for

bed. But is it all right if I call in in about ten minutes to say goodnight to James?'

'Of course,' Tom said. 'Come on, James.'

There was time for a few more minutes' chat with John. It was good to see him again, good to go over the good times that she'd had on the island. But after ten minutes she yawned and said she just had to go to bed. John accepted it quite happily.

In fact, James was already asleep when she tapped quietly on the door. But both Tom and herself knew that coming to see James had just been an excuse. Tom let her in, led her through the bedroom to the tiny lounge that looked out onto a balcony and then over the sea. They sat on a wicker couch, side by side in the semi-darkness.

'Seems a very nice chap, John Kersh,' Tom said, elaborately casual. 'A good man to work for.'

'He was good to work for and he was a friend to me. When I was here I went out with him a couple of times, just casually. But that was all. I was glad to see him again. But I have absolutely no wish to rekindle any kind of relationship. Because there never was one.'

'Good. But why are you telling me this?'

'Because it's something I want you to know. And you wanted to know. Didn't you, Tom?'

'I've got no rights about who your friends are. But, yes, I did want to know.'

He stretched his hand out, ran a finger down the side of her head, stroking her hair. It was a gentle caress, but she loved it. And she sensed that things were easier between them.

'There's a question,' he said. 'John said you had long hair, down to your shoulders. Why did you have it cut short?'

'You can guess the answer,' she said after a while. 'It was some kind of penance. And…James's hair dropped out so I felt I had to…'

'Now you know there's no need to be penitent. So will you let it grow again?'

'Yes,' she said. 'I think I will.'

He kissed her then. A soft, a gentle kiss. His arm slid round her back, he pulled her to him and their lips met very delicately. That was more than enough. To begin with. But then she felt his breathing deepen, felt something stir inside her that responded to him. His hold on her tightened. And at that moment there came a plaintive voice. 'Daddy…are you there?'

'He'll go to sleep in a minute,' Tom whispered to her. 'You can stay a while longer. We're still on holiday.'

It was an invitation that she would have loved to accept, but she shook her head. It would be too dangerous. 'We should go to sleep as well, Tom. This has been a long day and I've done and felt things that I thought were lost to me. But now I need to sleep.'

'I won't sleep. I'll think about you.'

She kissed him quickly. And as he moved to his son's bedside, she slipped out of the door.

He had been right when he'd said that he wouldn't sleep. As had happened so many times recently, his thoughts were in a turmoil. What should he do about Maria? Since she'd come to the clinic, his emotional life had been in chaos.

He had not been happy when she'd first come into his life. The memory of Jane had been too painful, even after four years. But with James he had worked out a pattern of living so that things hadn't been too bad. Then he'd met Maria. He had offered her a commitment that he'd never thought to offer again—and she'd rejected him. He had said that he was starting to love her and she had said that it was something he shouldn't say. Fair enough, perhaps. She'd had her reasons and she'd explained them. But then he'd begun to doubt her. When he'd seen how well she'd got on with James, he'd wondered if her phobia about children had only been a convenient excuse. She just didn't care for him that way.

They'd come on holiday together just as friends. They had slept together, on an afternoon that he knew he would never forget. But she'd been careful to tell him that this was a holiday—it meant there was no commitment.

And then there was John Kersh. Maria had said he was just a good friend, and Tom believed that she believed that was true. But he had seen a look in the man's eye. John Kersh was besotted by Maria. Maria obviously quite liked him. And now he, Tom, was jealous.

Tom was lost. Perhaps the best thing to do was distance himself from her. It was all too painful.

CHAPTER EIGHT

IT WAS on the plane going back that it finally happened. James was in the window seat, Maria in the middle and Tom by the aisle, where on occasion he could stretch out his long legs. James gazed out of the window.

But they didn't talk, they were content to sit. So much to think about. And it was in one of the quiet moments that it struck her. She loved Tom Ramsey. A proper, a true love. It wasn't just that she was attracted to him, it wasn't just that she liked his company, this was a real love that could stretch on for ever. The realisation came as a bit of a shock.

She should have known. Only yesterday she had given herself to him more fully than she had thought possible. But she'd not thought of the future. She'd told him that this was a holiday romance, that it would have no consequences. She had deceived him and also herself.

For over four years her life had been ruled by a sadness and fear out of her past, something that had made her flinch from much normal human contact. Now that fear had gone. She was free. And she loved Tom Ramsey.

So what did he feel for her? She wasn't certain. One thing she did know was that Tom would always want to do the right thing. And because they had been lovers, perhaps he would feel obliged…she didn't want him to feel obliged. Whatever feelings he had for her, she wanted them to be free, untrammelled by thoughts of what he ought to do.

He didn't know it but it wasn't a good time for him to interrupt her thoughts. She was still perplexed, not sure of what she wanted or how to get it. So she was thrown a little when a gentle voice beside her said, 'You're frowning, looking very thoughtful. If there's a problem, can I help you with it?'

She couldn't tell him what she really had been thinking. So she said, without considering the consequences, 'I was wondering about yesterday. About our holiday romance.'

He took a great breath, expelled it. 'I've been thinking about that, too,' he said eventually. 'After yesterday things are different. I feel that you are owed—'

That had been the wrong thing to say. She was instantly angry. 'Tom, I'm owed nothing! I told you that that was a holiday romance, that there was no commitment. And I meant it.'

'It's just that I feel…'

She glanced to her side. James was asleep but it would be only too easy to wake him. 'We can't talk about something like this on a plane, with your son sitting by my side,' she whispered frantically. 'But perhaps we ought to settle a few things. When can we meet?'

'Wednesday evening. Jeanette, the lady who'll be

looking after James, has to go to a school concert of some kind. Would you like to come round?'

'I'll come round after she's gone and James is asleep,' said Maria.

Monday, Tuesday and Wednesday work went on as usual. This surprised Maria. The stay in Majorca had changed her life completely. Why weren't other people affected by the change? But they weren't. For them the world hadn't altered. So she ran her clinics, saw the patients who came to see her individually and waited for Wednesday evening.

Their secret—if it was a secret—soon came out in the clinic. James told everybody in the crèche that he had been away to Majorca with Maria and Daddy. Well, it was to be expected. But no one commented, there were no snide remarks. Not that Maria would have cared if there had been. But if anything, the staff at the clinic seemed to be pleased.

And finally it was Wednesday evening. She waited until she was certain that James would be asleep, then went to Tom's house.

It was all right to kiss him when she got inside the house. They were friends, good friends. But it was she who gently eased him away. He had to make the first move.

'Come into the living room, Maria. I'll make some tea.'

He made the tea, didn't sit by her on the couch but took a seat opposite her. They were face to face. And his face was troubled.

'You look as if you're going to give me some bad news,' he said.

She had thought hard about this. She wanted him so much. But he had to be given every chance to make sure that anything he said was really, honestly, genuinely felt. She wanted no truck with his foolish ideas about honour or the right thing to do. He had to want her for herself.

'Not bad news,' she said. 'First I want to tell you that last week, when we made love, was wonderful and I'll never forget it. But I think it has to stop now. That was a holiday, this is the real world and to be lovers now just wouldn't do. We're back to where we were before, Tom, working together, being friends, but that's all.'

Somehow she managed to paste an insincere smile on her face. Desperately she hoped that he'd realise that she didn't mean it, that under this hard exterior was a softness that was meant only for him. He could argue with her, try to persuade her to change her mind. And she would change it.

But she had to give him that chance. And she remembered how, after they had made love for the first time and she had told him about her fears over James, he had been cold to her.

'So we're friends and nothing more?'

'We're friends. We work together.'

'Well, I suppose that's something,' he said. 'But I don't think it's entirely possible. Maria, we've been so close—you can't just forget about things like that. And you certainly can't ignore them. You either have to move on to some kind of long-term affair or you back off. And apparently you want to back off.'

'Probably the best thing,' Maria said. 'What do you think?' She fought to keep her voice casual, to make him think that she didn't much care whatever he decided. But it was hard.

He sighed. 'I guess it's friends, then,' he said, 'if that's what you want. You're not drinking your tea.'

For half an hour Tom sat in his living room, staring at the two cups of tea he had poured but seeing nothing.

After telling him that they were friends and nothing more, Maria had seemed to lose interest in drinking tea. In fact, she hadn't been able to get out of his house quickly enough. She had mumbled some excuse, almost run to the door.

Well, if she didn't want to stay with him, she didn't have to. But he just couldn't believe it. When they had made love it had been so much more than sheer animal passion. He had felt that when they were together that she was giving herself, her soul as well as her body. And he had wanted, had tried to do the same. It had been magic. And now this cold rejection. Friends who work together indeed!

Tom sighed. As well as a deep sadness, he felt a little anger. How could Maria give herself so completely and then say it was a holiday romance?

Perhaps she'd had holiday romances before? But he knew that thought was unworthy of him. He went and poured himself a brandy.

* * *

Maria had been—still was—happy in her little room in the nurses' home. She had added bits to the basic hospital furniture—a bright bedcover and cushions, pictures on the wall, the corkboard covered with postcards and photographs. It was homely. But as she returned there that night, she realised it was not enough.

She wanted a comfortable home like Tom's. She wanted a kitchen she could experiment in, not one she had to share. She wanted a large bedroom with a double bed, a living room with a real—well, nearly real—fire. Most of all, she realised, she wanted to go home to a family. To be greeted by someone who lived there and who loved her. The girls in the home were a good bunch, they were friends and they got on well together. But they were a poor substitute for a family.

Maria made herself the tea that Tom had made but she had not drunk. Probably because she had left so abruptly. Then she sat to think. Perhaps for the second time, her life seemed to be in ruins. Well, she would survive. She had done so before. What it would be like working for him, she just didn't know.

However, their first meeting after that passed well. Just a casual greeting in the corridor. 'I didn't drink my cup of tea last night,' she said cheerfully, 'No matter, I'll have it next time.'

'Yes,' he said hesitantly. 'Sorry. Any time.'

Maria smiled as she walked on. She had thrown him—it wasn't the reaction he had expected. Well, a bit of uncertainty might do him good.

An ante-natal clinic first. No real problems. Some

mums-to-be suffering from backache, some from digestive problems, some from sleeplessness. But all of them healthy and all of them looking forward to the birth with hope and pleasure. Sometimes she thought that being a midwife was the best job in medicine.

In the afternoon there was a post-natal clinic. This was another joyous assembly, but in quite a different way. The mums—not mums-to-be any more—had more to talk about.

Only when the second clinic was finished did she look over her records and frown. It was some time since she had seen Tracy McGee. She remembered that the girl had signed herself out of hospital after her partner had caused trouble in the ward.

She knew that Tracy must need help. She also knew that Tom had told her that they shouldn't interfere—that Tracy must be allowed to live her own life, make her own decisions. Well too bad. Tracy was going to get help whether she—or Tom—wanted it or not.

She knew, of course, that to a certain extent her actions were caused by an urge to get even with Tom, to prove to him that he wasn't always right. But Tracy did need help.

'Just going to make a local house call,' she said to Molly. She didn't, as she should have done, write down where she was going. She'd fill in the sheet when she returned.

The outside of the tower block was depressing. Rubbish blew all over, there were two burnt-out cars nearby. Tracy decided to drive past and park some distance away. Her car would be safer.

She grew even more doubtful when she entered the block. Graffiti was everywhere, even more rubbish piled up and a number of unpleasant smells. And the lifts didn't work. She stood for a moment and thought. She didn't have to do this. But then she set off to climb the stairs.

The next problem was finding Tracy's exact flat. Just which of these doors was hers? An older, care-worn-looking lady came down the stairs towards her. Maria said, 'I'm a midwife. I'm looking for Tracy McGee. Do you know which is her flat?'

The woman pointed at a door but then seemed worried. She surveyed Maria in her neat uniform, looked at the bag she was carrying. 'You don't want to go in there alone,' she whispered. 'Her fella—he can get a bit awkward at times. But don't say I told you.' Then she hurried on downwards.

Maria felt even less happy. But she'd come so far. Still…she took out her mobile phone, quickly tapped in the number of the clinic. 'I'm about to call at number 507 Dorian Towers,' she told Molly. 'It's the flat with the big black stain on the door. I'm calling on Tracy McGee. If I don't ring back in an hour, tell Tom, will you?'

'Maria, you shouldn't go there on your own. Wait until—'

'I'll be fine,' Maria said, and rang off. But she didn't feel fine.

She banged on the door. Someone inside shouted something—probably unpleasant—but the door wasn't opened. So she banged again. 'Midwife to see Tracy

McGee,' she called through the letterbox. This time the door was opened.

He looked just as she had feared. Dirty clothes, unshaven, a roll-up cigarette in his mouth and a definite smell—marihuana? 'Tracy don't want no midwife,' he said.

'She'll be giving birth soon, she needs to be examined. Look Mr…Mr…?'

'Lovett,' the man said.

'Mr Lovett, Tracy wasn't in a good way when you took her from hospital. If you're not careful, she and baby could be in considerable difficulties.'

'Difficulties?'

'Probably everything is fine. I'd like to find out. But there are dangers.'

The man appeared to consider. 'She is a bit poorly,' he said. 'But we're not going back to that hospital. I didn't like the way they treated me, as if I wasn't good enough for them. Come in, she's been asking for someone.'

Maria winced as she entered the room, tried not to look too hard at it. She was led through to a bedroom. A dirty double bed, rickety wardrobe and drawers, clothes on the floor. And a white-faced Tracy who didn't look at all good. But her face showed relief when she saw who it was. 'Maria, I think it's coming…' she moaned. The bed got all wet and I've got these pains and—'

'It can't be coming, Lovett snapped.

'Babies don't follow a timetable,' Maria said. 'Now, leave us alone for a minute. Go and boil some water,

I might need it.' In situations like this, telling people to boil water was the usual technique for getting rid of them.

Maria pulled on rubber gloves. She looked down at Tracy's face, which suddenly contorted in a grimace of pain. Maria felt under the bedclothes, laid a hand on Tracy's abdomen. That was a contraction all right. 'Your baby's going to be born,' she told the girl. 'Now, let's have a look at you.'

It only took half a minute to decide that this was not going to be a home birth. Tracy was in trouble. For a start, the lie wasn't right. And no way would she even try to bring a baby into the world in this mess.

Maria stepped out of the bedroom, closed the door. She took out her mobile phone and called Molly. 'Tell Tom that Tracy's in labour,' she said. 'She could need a Caesarean. We need an ambulance and—'

'Who d'you think you're calling?

He came out of what must be the kitchen door, as unpleasant as ever. 'Mr Lovett,' she said, 'there's a bit of a problem. Tracy just has to get to hospital. I'm phoning my boss to get him to arrange an ambulance and—'

'You're the midwife! You deal with it. Tracy isn't going into that place again.'

'She has to! I think she's—'

'I said you can deal with it. And you're not leaving here until you've finished.'

Maria had not been expecting violence, but suddenly he reached for her phone, grabbed it and threw it on the floor. Then he stamped on it. He pushed her towards the bedroom. 'If there's any trouble then you can sort it out. And if you don't, you'll have me to answer to!'

'Tracy could die!' Maria said. 'You don't understand, this is a real medical emergency and—'

There was a banging at the door. Not a polite knock, but the enraged banging of someone who intended to come in. And a voice shouted, 'This is Dr Ramsey. Open this door or I'll kick it in.'

Maria thought she'd never been more happy to hear his voice. She also thought she'd never heard him sound more angry.

Mr Lovett was too stoned or too stupid to recognise the anger. He called, 'You can go back to where you came from and—'

With a splintering crash, the door slammed open. In the doorway was Tom, white-faced with anger. He strode over to a quailing Mr Lovett and said, 'Stand by the wall and say nothing or I'll kick you right off the balcony. That isn't a threat, it's a promise.' He looked round, saw her, 'Maria, are you OK?'

'I'm fine, but Tracy's in real trouble. She's been in labour too long. We need an ambulance now!'

He walked into the room, took a quick glance at Tracy then took out his mobile phone and phoned 999. 'Ambulance, please. Can you get here quickly? Dr Ramsey calling, I've got an urgent case, birth imminent and the mother's in a very bad way. Thank you.'

Then there was a speedy examination and then he looked at Maria, his face grey. 'Nothing we can do here but wait and pray,' he said. 'We need Theatre. I'm going to call the hospital, get Mike Donovan standing by. In a minute you can go down to the front and tell the paramedics where to come.'

'OK.' This was an emergency, she should be thinking of her patient and nothing else. But… 'Tom, how come you got here so quickly? I'd only just phoned Molly and then you were kicking down the door.'

'I was already here,' he said. 'Molly told me where you were the minute you told her, and I came straight away. It was a stupid thing to do, Maria! I was worried about you!'

Just for once his voice was angry and she recognised he had every right to be angry. She didn't even mind being called stupid. 'Sorry,' she said contritely, 'I'll go and look out for the ambulance.'

A tiny part of her was pleased that Tom had worried so much.

Tom travelled with Tracy in the ambulance. Maria said she'd follow in his car, ring the clinic and make arrangements to have her own car picked up. She'd also ring Tom's mother, ask her to come to collect James. It might be quite a long wait. She was going to stay at the hospital. Tracy was her patient. If there was to be an operation then she wanted to be there to help, if possible.

Tracy was being prepped when she arrived. Tom and the team was scrubbing up. Maria asked if she could scrub up, too. When the baby was born she could be part of the team on take, could help resuscitate the baby if necessary, take it down to SCBU—the specialist care baby unit.

There was a full team working on Tracy's Caesarean with two surgeons, both Mike Donovan and Tom being there. And at first things seemed to be going fine. Tracy was stabilised, the baby was delivered, handed over to Maria's team, waiting patiently in the adjoining little theatre.

There was the usual Apgar test. The team had to look at colour, heart rate, muscle tone, breathing and stimulus response. Not too bad, a score of six out of ten. After an eventful birth, Tracy's new little boy seemed to be doing quite well. He was aspirated and ventilated, oxygen pumped into him to aid his breathing. Then he was settled into the portable incubator and Maria prepared to go with him down to SCBU. Just as they opened the door she heard a shout from behind. 'BP's rocketing!'

Maria hesitated. But the baby was her charge now, not Tracy. So, anxiously, she went down to SCBU.

Her help had been appreciated, but she wasn't part of the SCBU team, so there was now little for her to do. And she wanted to know how Tracy was. So she went back to Theatre. The operation was now over and Tracy had been transferred to ICU—the intensive care unit.

'What…what appears to be the trouble?' Maria asked the scrub nurse, who was now getting changed.

The scrub nurse shook her head wearily. 'I've never seen one before,' she said. 'It was frightening. Her BP rocketed, she started to drift away. It was Tom Ramsey who recognised what was happening. She had an amniotic embolism.'

'An embolism! Where's Tom now?'

'He's down in ICU with the girl. There's nothing more he or anyone else can do. Now it's just hope and chance. If she survives for the next three or four hours then she should pull through.'

An embolism! It just wasn't right. That it was the same condition that Tom's wife had died of. They were so rare, perhaps five a year in this country, and Tom had had to deal with two. Maria shuddered. She could only guess what he was going through.

She went down to the ICU, explained her interest in the case and was allowed in. Tracy was lying there, the bank of monitors by her bed measuring her progress. And sitting by the bed was Tom, his shoulders hunched, his head bowed.

Maria went over to him. She couldn't help herself. First of all she glanced at the monitors, checked on Tracy's condition. Tracy seemed to be holding her own, which was good. But with an embolism things could change in a minute.

Maria rested her arm on Tom's shoulder. He looked up in surprise, he hadn't heard her come in.

'There's not a lot you can do here,' she said. 'You know it's just waiting and hoping.'

'Then I'm going to wait and hope. Maria, there's James. I—'

'I've already phoned your mother, made arrangements for her to look after James. She'll stay the night with him.'

'You think of everything. What would I do without you?'

What could you do with me? she thought. But she said nothing.

Silently, they waited. Then slowly, almost imperceptibly, Tracy's vital signs improved. With an embolism it was pure chance. But after three hours Tracy could be said to be off the danger list.

It was the ICU staff nurse who eventually told Tom that he was wasting his time, that he was in the way of the staff and that with any luck Tracy should be fine. He could go home. If he wished, he could leave his mobile phone number and if there was any radical change in Tracy's condition she would phone him. So Tom came stumbling out of the room and stared, with unfocussed eyes, at Maria.

She took his arm. 'You can't go home looking like that,' she said. 'You'll worry your mother. Come to my room and I'll give you coffee and chocolate biscuits. If you want, you can have a shower.'

'All right,' he said.

So she took him to her room, sat him on her bed then went along to the kitchen to make coffee. The cold air as they walked across the grounds had revived him. And while she had been out of the room he had washed his face and hands and now looked more alert.

'Sorry to put you to all this trouble,' he said. 'Seeing another embolism, it took me back to Jane's death. I found that a bit...distressing.'

'Distressing? Is that all you can say?'

'These things happen,' he said.

Maria forced herself to keep her voice quiet. 'You've left yourself with no one to turn to, haven't you?' she said sadly. 'You're entirely alone. You even keep your mother at a distance, you won't talk to her about your feelings. You've cut yourself off—everyone knows you are the hard one, the one who copes.'

'That's the way I am. That's the way I deal with things.'

She sighed. 'Not always successful, is it? Look, kick your shoes off, lie down on the bed.' He looked startled at that, but did as she asked.

'You don't have to go home for a couple of hours,' she told him. 'What you need now is some live human contact.'

She lay by his side on the narrow bed, put an arm round his head so it rested on her shoulder. 'This isn't sex,' she told him. 'This is just warmth and comfort and…togetherness.'

She put her arms around him, gently held him. And slowly she felt the anger and the horror leave him, felt his stiff body relax. Neither said a word.

She wondered, as they lay there, just how honest she had been with him. Certainly she wanted to comfort him, as she would want to comfort any of her friends who were in this state. But there was more. She was trying to show him how rewarding having someone close could be. She wanted to show him just how wonderful it would be to share his bed with her.

She knew it was not an uncommon thing after moments of high emotion—for a while he slept. She lay by his side, for the moment perfectly content just to be with him. But then he woke, looked at his watch. 'I'd better go,' he said, 'Maria, I've taken up far too much of your time. And you've been so good to me.'

'You'd do the same for me,' she said, 'or for any friend. Wouldn't you?'

'Perhaps,' he said.

He reached down, slipped on his shoes. 'And where does this leave us?' he asked. I've slept with you again—but in a totally different way.'

'It leaves us as we were,' she told him steadily. 'Good friends.' Then, almost in desperation, she thought she was entitled to give him just the smallest of hints. 'If you ever want to change things, it's up to you.'

He leaned over to kiss her on the forehead. 'I don't deserve you, Maria,' he said.

You haven't got me, she thought. But I'd be yours if you wanted me.

CHAPTER NINE

NEXT morning there was another drop-in patient—Jan Casey. She was dressed all in black with dyed black hair, white make-up and a vast amount of mascara. Maria thought that she was barely sixteen.

'I'm a friend of Tracy McGee,' the teenager said. 'I went to see her in hospital last night. You know she's got a little boy and she's getting better?'

'I know. I've been to see her. I'm glad she's doing well.'

'Social Services have been to see her, too. They're going to get her a place away from that louse Lovett. She says she's got responsibilities now, she's going to clean her life up.'

'I think she'll manage it,' Maria said. 'Underneath, she's quite tough. Now, how can I help you Jan?'

'Yes, well...' The girl looked embarrassed. 'Tracy was telling me what you'd done for her, and how if I came here you'd look after me. I daren't tell me mam, and I won't go to that snotty doctor we've got.'

Maria sighed. 'How old are you?'

It took a while for the girl to reply. 'I'm nearly sixteen,' she said eventually.

'Nearly's not good enough. The law says that you are still a minor, that I ought to have your mother here with you.'

Maria saw the panic in the girl's eyes. 'I can't tell her. You won't, will you? Please, say you won't!'

'So far there's nothing to tell,' Maria said. 'Let me guess. You're pregnant?'

'Well, I might be. I could be, I suppose, I just don't know yet. I've felt a bit off recently, but that might be the drink I had. Isn't there a pill you can take, a morning-after pill?

'There is, but it's not always a good idea to take it. When did you last have sex?'

Maria thought that under the white pancake make-up Jan was blushing. She said, 'Well, actually, I've only done it once. Done it properly, that is. It was just a bit of fun. We met at a mate's house and had a few drinks and then…' Her voice trailed away.

'I know,' said Maria. 'Did you use any protection?'

'No. We got carried away. But we tried to be careful. A bit.'

Maria decided not to ask what being 'a bit careful' meant. She said, 'I asked you how long ago it was.'

Jan calculated. 'About ten days ago.'

'Well, there is a morning-after pill, but it's only effective up to about seventy-two hours afterwards, so it wouldn't help now. If you're not pregnant, we can look at different types of contraception.'

She took a sample jar from a drawer, gave it to Jan. 'Go next door and bring back a urine sample. If you can, take it in mid-flow. Then bring it back here.'

'Right,' said Jan. 'Does this mean that everything will be all right?'

'One step at a time,' Maria said.

The dipped-in stick didn't change colour, Jan wasn't pregnant. Maria hid a smile as Jan sighed with relief. Then the two looked at each other.

'I can't look after you, as Tracy suggested,' Maria said. 'You can only look after yourself. If you go around having unprotected sex then sooner or later you'll get pregnant.'

Maria studied the girl in front of her, wondered about what she was going to say, whether she felt happy with it or not. She could just send Jan away, her job had been done. But what about Jan's future? Was it her responsibility?

She made up her mind. 'You're fifteen,' she said. 'You're a minor. There's nothing I can do for you now. Only when you're sixteen does the law think that you're old enough to make up your own mind about whether you want to have sex or not. But that, of course, is up to you.'

'I'm thinking about it,' Jan said.

Maria knew there was no point in moralising, it would do little good. But she went on, 'And if you don't use protection, there's a chance you might get a disease.'

'Like Aids?' asked Jan.

'It's not impossible,' Maria said. 'But there are other diseases that are more common and almost as unpleasant. There's urethritis, chlamydia, gonorrhoea. They're all hard to get rid of.' She looked doubtfully at Jan.

Maria sighed, then phoned Molly and said she would be busy for the next half-hour.

'I'm going to talk to you about contraception, safe sex and sexually transmitted diseases,' she said to Jan. 'I've got leaflets here, too. Take them away and read them. But always remember, when it comes to sex, you're the one making the decisions. I'm not telling you what to do. I'm just telling you how to avoid trouble.'

Half an hour later Jan left. Maria sat and wondered. At least Jan was now better informed.

'I think that finishes the official business,' Tom said, shuffling a pile of papers straight on his desk. 'Have you time for a coffee before you get back to work?'

About once a week Tom and Maria had a meeting to discuss outstanding cases, consider requisitions for the next few months, decide on policies for the future. It was one of the things that made him a good boss. He consulted. Maria, and all the other people who worked for him, felt that they were partners, they were helping in the decision-making.

'I'll skip the coffee,' she said. 'I am busy. But is there anything else you want to bring up?' Then she remembered his words. They'd finished the official business. Were they going to talk about something personal?

It was now five days since he had watched over Tracy and then come to rest on her bed. Tracy was now recovering and her baby was doing well. Maria had been to see her and had been heartened by the visit. Tracy seemed filled with determination that she was going to start a new life. Maria was pleased that people who had started by making a mess of their lives could in time recover.

Tom had not mentioned his stay in her room. Rather bitterly, Maria decided that he wanted to forget his…weakness?

And now he looked decidedly uneasy.

'You know my mother's in Australia and I've got Jeanette, this rather good ex-nurse, looking after James when I can't?'

Maria nodded. 'Of course I know. James had a card from your mother, he brought it to show me.'

'Well, I've got an important meeting on Friday that may last well into the evening and it's a night that Jeanette can't come. Some family business. So I wondered—and it was James who suggested it—if you would come and be babysitter for a night. I might be very late, you'd have to sleep over.'

Maria looked at the blond hair that had brushed her face as they'd made love. She looked at the impenetrable face, its expression guarded as ever. Why did she bother with this man?

Because she loved him. And she'd do whatever he asked, no matter what it cost her.

'I'll come and babysit,' she said. 'I've quite missed James. What time do you want me?'

It was odd, going back to his house. His meeting lasted well into the evening, so she took James home and gave him his tea. After watching a video, she took him upstairs for his bath. She was playing at being a mother, at being the lady of the house whose husband was away for a while. And though it was painful, she enjoyed it.

It was fun, kneeling by the bath, clad in one of the long pinafores that Tom's mother had left her. The bath was filled with bubbles, she wound up his clockwork submarine and James squealed with delight as it made its slow progress through the foam.

She put him to bed, read him a story and sat with him until he fell asleep. Then she went down to the kitchen to make her own supper, and felt more lonely than she had ever done in her life.

Tom had made up a bed for her in James's bedroom as before. She just couldn't settle. When finally she did manage to doze off it was a broken sleep that brought no respite at all. She sighed, sat up. Perhaps a warm milk drink might help her. Anything was better than this.

She slipped out of the bedroom, dressed only in a flimsy nightdress and dressing-gown, and gasped as she nearly walked into Tom. They stood, face to face, almost, almost touching. All he was wearing—apparently—was a black silk dressing-gown. She remembered he had told her that he hated wearing anything in bed. And when they had slept together, both had been naked.

'I thought I heard James calling,' he said. 'I was just coming to look.'

She wondered if this was true or if he had come to look at her. But she said, 'Of course. I was going to get myself some milk.' He didn't move and neither did she.

For perhaps a minute they stood there and she stared deep into those cerulean blue eyes. They were fixed on her with so much longing, and she knew that her own eyes betrayed the same message.

'Would you like a drink?' she asked.

'No, thank you. I've just had one. Goodnight, Maria.'

Then they both moved on. The words they'd exchanged had been simple, ordinary. They had hidden what both of them were feeling. But it had been up to him to make the first move. And he hadn't.

She didn't sleep much the rest of that night. She tried to be neither angry nor sad. She decided that she had been far too emotional over the past few weeks, now it was time to look at her life coldly and logically.

First of all she remembered the job offer from John Kersh. She had loved living and working in Majorca and now she was at ease with herself over James's death, she felt she could return there. Her Spanish was as good as ever. She knew she could do the job. She could start a whole new life. Again.

But what was wrong with this life? She loved the work, she had a future in it, she had friends to support her, she had everything she needed except… Now she had to face up to the brutal facts.

She was in love with Tom. Absolutely, overwhelmingly, completely in love with him. But he didn't or couldn't or wouldn't love her.

Well, she could stand it no more. More happiness now would only lead to more misery later. She'd tell him next week. She would be sorry to leave him but she was leaving the clinic and going back to the main hospital. She had that right. And then she would hand in her resignation. She would leave the hospital, too.

CHAPTER TEN

TRACY McGEE looked well. Her face had filled out a little, her hair shone, looked well brushed. She wasn't wearing quite so many metal studs and the ex-army overcoat had gone. She looked tired but content. And every five minutes she glanced down with pride at the little form in the pram by her side.

'I've stopped doing drugs,' she told Maria. 'I've got this great little flat and I'm going to keep it a lot better than the last place. I'm starting a new life.'

'It's going to be hard,' Maria said, 'but I bet you can do it.'

Tracy nodded. 'Just watch me.' She pointed at the pram. 'I've got Oliver now. Responsibilities. And next summer I'm going to start a course at the local tech. A foundation course, they call it.'

'You've got your life planned.' Maria hesitated a minute. 'But what about your boyfriend—Mr Lovett? Is he part of your new life?'

Tracy looked a little sad. 'Andy? I've kicked him into touch. I want to change my life, he doesn't. Comes down to a choice between him and Oliver. So I picked Oliver.'

'You're sorry to lose him?

Tracy shrugged. 'I guess I am. I know he loved me in his own way and I suppose I loved him. But for me and Oliver to be all right he had to go. So I kicked him out and I won't have him back.'

There was a toughness, a resolution in Tracy's voice that Maria could only admire.

It wasn't going to be an easy conversation. Still, she had made up her mind. Although she managed to smile and pretend that nothing had changed, she knew that things were no longer the same. There was a coldness in her, a grim determination to get out of a situation that could only end in more misery for her. And she thought of Tracy McGee. If she could turn her world around—leave the man she thought she loved—then so could Maria.

She went to Tom's room late that afternoon. 'I'm afraid we need to talk,' she told him.

He sighed, put down the forms he had been reading. 'I suppose we do,' he said, 'I've been expecting this all day.'

This shocked her. 'You've been expecting it? Why?'

His smile was sad. 'We've worked together for a while now, Maria. I can tell when something's on your mind. You frown more. And you don't answer straight away when someone speaks to you, you're obviously thinking about something else.'

'I see.' She hadn't realised that she was so transparent—or that he was so observant.

There was no way of making this conversation easy, she said what she had to say at once. 'I want to leave the clinic and go back to the hospital,' she said. 'I believe I have that right.'

She could tell he was shaken. But he remained calm. 'We'd be very sorry to see you go,' he said. 'Can you tell me why? Can we talk things through? I thought you were happy here.' Then he frowned. 'You're not thinking of going to Majorca, are you?'

Her patience snapped. Her determination to be cool, distant, perfectly reasonable—it all disappeared. 'No, it's not John's offer of a job,' she snapped, 'though I shall probably take it up and I'll enjoy it. It's because I'm not happy here.' Then she said it. 'Tom, I'm not happy with you. For me you're just too calm, too self-contained. There's a nice person hiding in you, but when it comes to feelings, you don't really give anything away. It's your way but it's not mine.'

'But, Maria, I—'

'It's too late,' she said.

He felt empty as he went to bed that night. A life without Maria would be hard to face. And James would be desolate.

It had not been all that easy. He was constantly aware of her, couldn't stop thinking of the twice they had made love. He loved the swell of her breasts, the curve of her lips, the colour of her hair. He loved everything about her. Sometimes the urge to just grab her, hold her, was more than he could bear. But he'd managed.

But it was more than that. They just fitted so well together. Their ideas, the way they worked, sometimes their very words were the same. Maria was the other half of him.

He thought back on their times together, not only the two wonderful times they had made love but also the sheer pleasure of just being with her. And then he remembered the one—in fact, the two times—he had hesitantly told her that he loved her. The morning after their first night together and days later on the promenade. Each time she had rejected him, and the pain had been so great that he had vowed never to risk it again. He was his own man. Love offered was always a risk.

Of course, if she'd shown any sign that she really cared for him—loved him even—things would have been different. He'd take any risk then. But each time they'd been close she'd made it more than clear that she didn't want any further involvement.

Perhaps he did appear to be a taker rather than a giver. But if she'd given him a chance he'd have given her all of him. But it was her right to choose. She didn't love him. Well, that was clear enough. He'd just have to manage without her. Still, it would be hard on him.

Maria didn't want to leave the clinic. She had made friends there, she had developed her own way of working, she had her own responsibilities. Back at the hospital she'd be just one of a large number of midwives. Here she enjoyed being the only midwife.

And she loved working with Tom. But that was the reason that she'd have to leave. She'd been strong so far. But she knew that strength would weaken. So she left quickly, quietly, saying goodbye to no one.

'We can manage somehow,' Jenny told her when she went for a talk. 'I've got another midwife who'll be pleased to take your place in the clinic, though she won't be as good as you. And I can always use you here.'

'So it's all right, then?'

'Not entirely.' Jenny tapped a letter on the desk in front of her. 'I've got your resignation from the hospital here. I want you to take it back.'

Dully, Maria shook her head. 'It's no good, Jenny. I can't be happy here. I need to move on.'

'I'll put the letter to one side, not act on it yet. Things might seem different in a couple of weeks.'

'They'll seem worse. I'm managing now because I'm doing something, I'm taking control of my life, making decisions. But I know the decisions won't make me happy.'

'I remember that feeling.' Jenny looked closely at her friend. 'Do you want to tell me what happened? I thought you were getting close to Tom again.'

'I did have hopes but they came to nothing. He just can't care for me. Jenny, I could have made him so happy! But he's still carrying round this huge burden of fear.'

'I thought he was coming out of that.'

'He was!' Maria said, trying to stop the tears. 'He…he offered me a chance. He did once say that he thought that he was falling in love with me. I turned him down and that made him even harder than ever.

He said that he'd never mention it again and he never has.'

'Have you tried talking to him? Suggesting that you might have changed your mind?'

'It has to come from him. He knows that I get on with James now, he knows that I've lost my fear of being with children. But he can't stand the idea of loving someone and then losing them. And now we're both feeling worse than before. And I hate abandoning that little boy. But...I couldn't stand it any longer, Jenny.'

'Tom showed no sign of changing his mind when you said you'd leave?'

'He didn't move an inch,' said Maria.

For some reason she didn't write to John Kersh. She was too despondent. The job was there when she needed it, she'd write in a week or two.

Fortunately, she had her work to keep her engrossed. She was much less her own boss in the hospital and she missed the more intimate atmosphere of the clinic. But she was still a midwife and she took joy in the babies she helped be born, the happiness of her patients.

There was one phone call from Tom. 'Just to check up that you're all right,' he said. 'We're all missing you here. No way we can tempt you back?'

What a question to ask! 'I'm surviving,' she said. 'Goodbye, Tom.'

She'd volunteered to work the night shift. It was longer, it filled her time and she was always able to sleep during the day. And she didn't really want to mix with anyone. She was happiest when she was working.

In fact, she had just finished a night shift and was soundly asleep when someone knocked on her door. It was a loud, a purposeful knock. Someone intended to come in, whether she wanted them to or not.

She dragged herself awake, stared at the clock by her bed. Ten o'clock? She'd barely been asleep for two hours. And all the other girls knew she was working nights, they'd take special care not to disturb her.

There was more knocking on the door.

She staggered out of bed, put on her dressing-gown. It was Jenny at the door. And she looked upset.

'What…?' Maria mumbled.

Jenny stepped forward, eased Maria back into the room so she sat on the bed.

'I know you've just come off nights,' she said. 'But I've just been told something and I thought you'd want to know.'

Maria blinked, wondering what was so important that it couldn't wait until she was awake. 'What?' she mumbled.

Even in her sleepy state she could tell that Jenny was upset. And by the way Jenny was looking at her, she was worrying about upsetting her even more. Maria started to feel anxious.

Jenny rested a hand on Maria's arm. 'James Ramsey was brought into A and E late last night. It was an RTA. Tom had parked his car, and got out to help

James out of his car seat. A van was driving past, apparently a front tyre burst and the van skidded and crashed into the back of the car, where James was strapped in. And James was hurt.'

Maria stared at her friend, trying desperately to comprehend the horror of what she had just heard. 'How badly hurt?' she managed to gasp at last.

'Pretty badly. His chest was slashed by a spike of metal and he has a double fracture of the humerus. They're bad enough in such a young child, but they can be dealt with. The worst is the head injury, James had intracranial bleeding. In fact, he had something rather rare, he had an extradural haemorrhage.'

'What does that mean for James?'

'Fortunately, we had a surgeon available, and he operated at once. This is something that has to be treated quickly. He relieved the pressure on the brain, there's now good chance that James will...will survive.'

It's happening again, Maria thought, another child that I...that I love might die. 'Where is James now?'

'He's in the intensive care unit and Tom's with him. But he knows there's nothing he can do but wait and hope.'

'I want to go to him. Jenny, can you find a replacement for my shift tonight?'

'I've already done it,' said Jenny. 'Now I'll fetch you a coffee while you get dressed.'

Maria glanced at the bank of instruments and dials that stood by the side of the bed holding the little form. She shuddered. James's condition was critical. She looked down at his still body—and then looked at Tom.

He was wearing one of the suits that he usually wore to work, only the tie had been loosened. He was sitting staring at his son as if simple desperation could help James survive. Then he felt her presence and looked up at her.

His voice was calm. 'Hello, Maria, what are you doing here?'

Her first reaction was rage. How could he ask such a senseless question? But then she forced herself not to get angry. Apparent calmness was Tom's way of coping with the world. She knew him. She knew what he was feeling. Still, she was entitled to remind him that other people had feelings.

'I'm here because I've come to love James. And I'm here to offer you any support that I can. How…how is he progressing?'

She wondered what was worse, being a layman who knew little about the medicine or being someone who knew the meaning of every alteration in James's condition.

'Look at the readings. He can't carry on like this, his body won't stand it. I think the next four or five hours will be critical. If he can get through those then he stands a chance of recovery. He's in the same situation as Tracy McGee. Or Jane. It could go either way.'

She couldn't speak then, the sheer horror of it all swelled within her. And how could he speak so dispassionately? This was his son he was talking about. But, then, that was Tom's way.

She bent to hug him, kissed his cheek. Perhaps a little human warmth might comfort him. His face was rough against hers. 'How long have you been here?' she asked.

'All night. I drove him to A and E myself, even though the car was wrecked. I phoned ahead as I drove. It was all a bit…horrific.'

At last, a touch of feeling!

'I'll sit here now. Why don't you go and find somewhere where you can shave and shower, change into scrubs and get something to eat and drink? Have you had anything yet?'

'I've had a couple of coffees. Sister brought me a sandwich but I couldn't eat it.'

'Your blood sugar must be at rock bottom. Get something inside you. Tom, you're no good to James in this state! You need to be strong! You've got your bleep. If there's any change at all, I'll get straight onto you.'

He looked at her, it was the first time she had seen his face closely. There were the obvious lines of fatigue round his eyes and mouth. He could keep his voice calm, but there was no way he could disguise the fear and desperation in his face.

It took him a while to reply, as if he had difficulty in working out what she was saying. 'As ever, Midwife Wyatt is right. I'll do as you say. You have got my bleep number?'

'Just go,' she said. 'I suppose it's no use suggesting that you try to sleep for a couple of hours?'

'No use at all,' he said.

He was back in twenty minutes, and perhaps he did look a little better. Before speaking to Maria, he checked the readings again. No change. 'You were right,' he said, 'I don't feel better but I do feel stronger.' He looked down. 'You've fetched another chair,' he said.

'I'm going to sit with you.'

'It's good of you, but you don't really need to. I can cope now and…'

It was hard to whisper and shout at the same time, but she managed it. 'Tom Ramsey, if I hear you talking about coping again, I think I'll hit you! One, I'm here because of James. Two, I'm here because I think that, just a little, me being here might help you. And I want to help you because…well, I just do.'

She had intended to say 'because I love you'. But at the moment he had enough to deal with, without the expression of an unwanted love.

They sat together. The needles on the dials twitched just a little. James stirred and moaned. This was a crisis. Perhaps *the* crisis.

The sister came in, looked down at James and then a moment later the paediatric consultant entered. He looked at the monitors, thought for a moment then gripped Tom's shoulder. 'You know what's happening?' he asked gruffly.

'We should know if he's going to live or die within the next hour or so,' Tom said.

The consultant looked taken aback by this bald statement. 'Well, yes,' he said. 'I'll be on the ward next door if there's any…radical alteration.'

Tom and Maria sat in silence. Perhaps the needles quivered again. She reached for his hand and grasped it, managed not to wince at the strength of his grip. And they watched. Looked at the little boy lying in the bed, looked at the dials.

The needles quivered again. And slowly, so, so slowly they stared to creep back to normal. The sister came in, this time with a broad smile on her face. 'Looks like good news, doesn't it?' she said cheerfully. 'If we carry on with this progress. I'll just nip next door and tell the consultant, he'll be pleased.'

Ten minutes later the consultant came in, he, too, with a broad smile. 'I think the panic is over,' he said. 'His condition is still serious, but it's not dangerous any more. Tom, find a bed somewhere and go and get some sleep. You look a mess. Stay in the hospital. If there's any relapse, I'll bleep you. But my professional opinion is that there won't be. This is a strong little lad.'

Tom stood, looked puzzled, as if he didn't quite know what to do.

'You're coming with me,' Maria said. 'You can sleep in my room again. No way are you going to be alone.'

It was late afternoon, shadows were lengthening. They walked across the hospital grounds without speaking and she took him straight to her room. 'Nothing is more tiring than extreme emotion,' she told him.

'I know it, and you know it, too. So don't argue, don't think. You don't even need to get undressed. Just get into bed.'

'But what if—?'

'If there's any news, I'll wake you.'

He tumbled into bed. A moment late he was asleep.

Maria was tired, too, and wondered if there'd be enough room for the two of them on her narrow bed. There had been when she brought him here after he'd looked after Tracy, but this was different. She sat in her easy chair, put up her feet on another chair and within minutes she was also asleep.

Tom was awake before her. Her eyes flicked open. He was leaning over her, still in his scrubs. At once she remembered what he was doing there, why they were together. 'James?' she asked.

'James is doing fine. Half an hour ago I slipped out of your room, phoned the ward. Sister there says that he's making a great recovery and for the moment we can stop worrying.'

'Didn't you want to go over there to see him? If you didn't want to wake me, you could have left me, phoned me later with any news. You know I want to know how he is.'

'I know that. In fact, in a few minutes we can go over to see him together. I'd like it if you came with me.'

She was struggling to wake up, struggling also to make sense of Tom. The sleep he'd had—it could only have been three or four hours—seemed to have revived him miraculously. The lines of strain were gone from his face. The old calm Tom was back, the man who was in control of his emotions. And she had the weirdest idea…

'Why did I wake up just then?' she asked. 'Did you shake me or something?'

'No. I kissed you.'

She had thought so. But her conscious mind had told her that it had probably been a dream. It had been a very pleasant dream, perhaps some kind of wish fulfilment. But he had kissed her. 'You shouldn't really kiss people when they're asleep,' she said. 'It's…it's harassment.'

'You can kiss people when they're asleep if you love them,' he said.

Then he looked at her as if afraid of what she might say.

Maria shook her head, struggling to make sense of this. 'If you love them?'

'That's what I said.'

'You mean you love me?'

'It's taken me a while to realise it. It's taken me even longer to grab the courage to tell you. But, yes, Maria, I love you.'

She stood, wobbled slightly. 'Sit on my bed and don't go away,' she said. 'We need to talk and I need to be awake. You love me?'

He sat on her bed. 'No one could love you more.'

Maria went to her little bathroom, ran water into the washbasin and rinsed her face. The shock woke her completely. She peered into her mirror and groaned. She looked a mess!

Still, Tom didn't seem to mind.

He'd said he loved her! She was still tired, she was entitled to be. But in spite of her fatigue she could sense a new feeling growing. Her life was going to change! There was fresh hope in her. Suddenly the world seemed full of so many possibilities that she couldn't begin to count them. He loved her! Perhaps she'd better go out and tell him that she loved him, too.

He stood as she came out of the bathroom, wrapped his arms around her and kissed her. Perhaps for both of them it was a still-tired kiss, but from it she took so much joy, so much hope. This was like coming home.

She didn't know how long they stood there, but eventually she eased him away, though not too far. She mumbled, 'I love kissing you and I want to do it for ever. But first I want to talk to you. Or I want you to talk to me. Do you know, Tom Ramsey, that I've loved you… Well, I nearly told you how much I loved you on the plane, coming back from Majorca.'

He looked astounded. 'You did? Maria, I never knew! I thought that you…well, you didn't care for me that way.'

'And I thought that you were a clever man.'

He sat on her bed, pulled her down so that she was leaning next to him, his arms round her shoulders, her cheek against his. 'I want to be serious,' he said.

'Just for a minute. And then you can kiss me again.'

'Serious just for a minute, then.'

He couldn't speak for a moment. She put her arms around his waist and squeezed him. 'I'm a doctor,' he said. 'I knew the risks only too well and I knew that James could die.'

'It's over, Tom. James is recovering.'

'I know. But I went through the same feelings I had when Jane died. What if I lost him, too?'

'Tom, it didn't happen! And it won't now. Stop thinking about it.'

'That's what I've got to do,' he said, 'and with you I think that's what I can do.'

He did kiss her then, but quickly. 'I think I've loved you since that first time we met. Leaning over that old man who had been knocked down. Later on I could see that you had problems and I took it on myself to help you. A bit arrogant, wasn't it?'

'You did help me! You got me my life back.'

'I didn't realise I was doing it as much for me as for you. I wanted to be near you, to do things with you. I didn't realise that I was falling in love, and when I did, I was terrified.'

It was her turn to kiss him. 'After Jane that was understandable,' she said.

'Not really. Because just now, when I woke up and you were still asleep, after I'd phoned the ward, it all seemed clear to me. All life is a risk. I'd be a fool to turn down infinite happiness with you just because something might go wrong. It won't go wrong. Why should it? So, Maria…I love you. I want to share my life with you. What do you say?'

'Can I move back in with you tomorrow?'

'You can move back in with me for ever,' he said.

By Heather Graham, Lindsay McKenna, Marilyn Pappano and Annette Broadrick
On sale 18th November 2005

By Marion Lennox, Josie Metcalfe and Kate Hardy
On sale 2nd December 2005

By Margaret Moore, Terri Brisbin and Gail Ranstrom
On sale 2nd December 2005

By Lisa Jackson, Barbara Boswell and Linda Turner
On sale 18th November 2005

1105/XMAS/LIST 2a